RATS: A TRAGEDY OF TIMELINE TOURISM

JH Tomen

ISBN:
ISBN-13: 979-8-9862909-8-0

For my mother.
Your love was a golden, precious thing.
It made me, placing a spark in my heart I still can't put out.

All of this really happened. Sort of.

Even if it's in a made-up, sci-fi vessel, this story deals with my
Mom's real-life suicide. Not a day goes by that I don't wish she
was here.

If you or someone you know is experiencing suicidal thoughts
or a crisis, please call the Suicide Prevention
Lifeline at 988 or text HOME to the Crisis Text
Line at 741741. These services are free and confidential.

et tui amóris in eis ignem accénde
renovábis fáciem terræ

Cover by Karl Nilsson (@sigvardnilsson)
Edits by Joe Pierson

1

I guess you never really know what to expect when traveling to your own past. I didn't, anyway. The memories I had were strange, brittle things — more shapes than pictures. Being here in person, though, I hardly recognize what I'm seeing. I'm in the back of a minivan, a concrete parking structure rising up around me. It feels strange to be buckled in a back seat. Strange to be a child again. Is this what the world looked like? What it *felt* like?

I remember the van, of course. It's always been a sort of awful talisman in my mind, more symbol than vehicle. And in that sense, even if I don't remember everything from this day, I still feel this memory in my bones. The realness of it, the coming tragedy. All of it is etched onto my soul. All these years later, and I still haven't managed to let go. I think part of me will always be stuck in 2002.

I suppose that's why the scientists picked me for the experiment. "Emotional anchoring," they called it. Part of me wants to cry — both sad and happy tears — so overwhelmed am I to be in this place I thought I'd lost forever. If time is a circle, then this is like riding a Ferris wheel. I just don't know whether I'm at the top or the bottom yet.

"You won't be able to cry, you know," my AI chirps in my head. "Remember your training. I'm your guardrails, here to help you select from a range of timeline-coherent responses."

Right, I think back at the thing, my tongue unable to move just yet. The tone in my mind is a bit snappier than I intended, though it's not like the bot has feelings. I've learned that the hard way. As the scientists stressed over and over again in training, the chip in my head is more hall monitor than friend. *Robotic-Amni-Temporal-Stability-Unit-7*, I've taken to calling him RATS — something that seemed to bother the scientists very deeply. The AI may have empathy sensors, but his programs have one purpose — to make sure I don't destroy the timeline.

But then, I hear it. *Her voice.* It makes all the anger melt away, threatening to bring on a river of tears mightier than the Mississippi. My mom. She opens the driver's side door of the van, climbing in behind the steering wheel.

"So?" she asks. "Do you still wanna see that Spider-Man movie?"

Visuals from RATS start flashing in my HUD. Most of it is unintelligible — charts and graphs used for optimal timeline consistency — but among them are word-based prompts. The first is what I actually said when this memory happened — or at least as close as the AI can tell by processing my timeline's quarks. The others are things I *could* say if I want to, things close enough to timeline-accurate so as not to throw off all of human history. It's a delicate balance, this timeline tourism — though I'm more than happy to be their guinea pig. I'll certainly never be able to afford what they plan on charging future customers.

"You need to speak," RATS says. It's an order, a countdown timer appearing in my left eye. Saying nothing can sometimes be an option, but in this case, my mom is looking at me in the rearview mirror, every millisecond integral to timeline integrity. Unfortunately, I also learned through my training that RATS will speak for me if I don't do my part. I'm just so...*awestruck*. This is the woman I've spent such an impossible time missing, and she's right in front of me. This is so much more than a picture. She's...right...*here*.

I will, I think at RATS, feeling like a snarky child. Physically, I *am* a child, at least on the outside. In this memory, I'm eleven, even if they've managed to preserve my adult self in the AI's memory simulacrum.

"Sounds great," I say to my mom, picking one of the options from the list.

Can you get rid of this shit? I can't think with all these graphs. Just give me the text options and the countdown, alright?

"Yes, sire," RATS says in a butlery voice.

Was that...a joke?

"Yes. I'm capable of many things."

I suppose they *had* warned me about RATS. In the words of the scientists, they would "sculpt him from my own personality to ensure total mission success." He's a sort of back door into my mind, something to keep me compliant as I play around with time. All's fair in love and time war, I suppose. Besides, his snark *does* work. Part of me feels strangely shamed, even if I was only being rude to what amounts to a mouthy stopwatch.

I'll be more polite next time. Thanks, RATS.

He harrumphs in my mind, but there's no way I'm dropping the nickname. After all, I have to keep some kind of upper hand on this thing. Anyway, it hardly matters, at least not compared to what I'm witnessing. My mom, driving me to a movie. Even something as boring as her hands on the steering wheel is suddenly the most beautiful thing I've ever seen. Was this how she drove? Was this what it felt like to be carted around Detroit? I mean, what could be better than this?

Of course, I'm also trying to forget the bad memories I have of this van. The reasons it's so mythic, so...*totemic*. I wrote songs about this van, drew it in art school, talked about it in therapy. I might be an old man in my own timeline, but this midnight blue Chrysler Town & Country lives on inside me. And it's only now that I realize — *truly* realize — why RATS is here to watch me. Seeing my mom, hearing her, being even remotely *near* her. Without this AI hijacking my brain, there's no way I wouldn't try to save her.

2

The movie is easily the most surreal experience of my life. *Lives?* Whatever. With every movie moment happening so quickly, RATS has decided he can't trust me with a timer. He's taken full control of my body, shunting me into the back seat of my mind as the story unfolds. I'm oohing and aahing involuntarily, forced to relive the first time I saw the movie. You'd think it doesn't matter how a kid reacts to Sam Raimi's *Spider-Man*, but what do I know about the spacetime continuum?

Thankfully, it's not an altogether unpleasant experience. It's sort of fascinating in a way, reliving a physical memory — the goosebumps on my skin, the way my heart pounds. If this is temporal tourism, it's of the immersive variety, granting me the closest thing possible to the *real* thing. Besides, I really did love this movie. Between *Spider-Man*, *Hey Arnold*, and *Harry Potter*, my entire personality was built over just a handful of summers. Unfortunately, those characters will also weave my self-loathing with a potent hero complex — the kind that makes old men sign up for lab experiments.

But today, none of that has happened — yet. There's a freedom in that. My adult memories, while *technically* accessible through the neural tether, are sort of vague in this time and space. So, I let them go, dropping into the River Styx and the thrill of sitting in a movie theater with my wonderful, quirky, insane beauty of a dead mother. What more could an octogenarian in a child's body ask for?

Mom's eyes are glowing, reflecting the flashing lights from the giant movie screen. I stick my hand in the popcorn tub — and try to relish even being allowed to eat the buttery magic, something my future dentists will stop allowing in my thirties. I may not be a paying customer on this experiment, but they gave me a ticket, and I plan on punching it.

"So?" Mom asks, one arm wrapped around me as we ride the escalator down after the movie. "What did you think?"

Thankfully, RATS has given me my body back, though it's still hard to focus. My body is completely unused to being hugged, to the feeling of absolute safety.

I'm suddenly dying for more, desperate to regain the love and attention I spent my whole life missing. I want to bury my face in her shirt and cry — her past self still towering over me despite how short she was. But a tween wouldn't cling to his mom, right? I'm forced to act natural, selecting one of the answers from the HUD.

"It was *so* cool," I say, my mouth curling into an automated grin. "I wish I had webs like that."

I look out the window, presumably imagining myself swinging between the buildings — though RATS doesn't display any daydreams in my mind. They tried to explain this to me during my training briefings. It has something to do with the way tachyons travel through time. Through subatomic imaging, the AI can track my words and actions closely enough, but RATS can't actually know what was going on in my head at the time. I'll never *fully* replicate the experience of being a child.

Still, it's a nice view — or a nostalgic one, anyway. We went to the Palladium, the fancy new theater in Birmingham designed like a Parisian arrondissement for no apparent reason. In our wealthy little suburb of Detroit, a consortium of doctors and lawyers had colluded to be as gauche as humanly possible. It's still a cute place, though, and picture perfect in its own way. Plenty of trees, a tiny walkable downtown. And on the blocks where the mid-century ranches haven't been knocked down for McMansions, it's downright charming.

It took time to build all this perspective. I didn't know a lick of history when I was eleven, ignorant to the fact that Detroit had basically invented White Flight. With factories churning out automobiles and the highways going in, a very pernicious sort of racism took hold. The city paved through Black Bottom, a thriving black business district, to build I-75. The white folk then used that same roadway to "escape" their fellow countrymen after the '68 uprising. But at eleven, this place can just be beautiful, a paradise of greenery and time spent with my mom.

Besides, Detroit turned out alright in the end, didn't it? After all, it never lost its thriving Black culture. And with the robotics boom of the 2040s, it will be almost as if the white elite hadn't spent a century divesting every penny they could from the place. Sure, the sports teams are still owned by a bunch of slum lords, but Detroit found its way despite every albatross we hung around its neck. Like Joe Louis, the city got up from the mat and kept fighting. For the first time, I feel genuinely grateful for RATS being plugged into my brain. After all, if he allowed me to alter my past, couldn't it destroy Detroit's future?

"You know," my mom says, bringing me back to the past-present moment, "I went to college with the movie's director. He asked me to be in *Evil Dead*. But he said I had to play the girl who has sex with the tree, so I said no."

My mom was always wildly inappropriate, but not in a devious way. She was just overly honest, a trait I picked up myself — albeit without her…bipolar flair. Full disclosure was simply her way. She seemed to think my brother and I were full people — which, of course, we were in a way. She never felt the need to hide things from us or water life down.

And honestly, after fifteen years of repression and Catholic school, she still feels like a breath of fresh air. It's not like her story about Sam Raimi turned me into a tree-sex lunatic. If anything, it gave me a certain open-mindedness I still have today. Not that anything she told us would have passed muster with the PTA. A year after this memory, when I tell her I'm getting bullied, she'll tell me about the tiny penis my bully's father had. Apparently, she heard about it from a friend of hers who had an affair with the guy. A totally appropriate secret to tell a twelve-year-old.

"Anyway, what do you think the movie was trying to say? What about that responsibility thing?"

With great power comes great responsibility. Honestly, my tiny brain was absolutely *magnetized* by the movie. But as we stepped off the escalator and my mom pulled us to the side to hear my answer, I was struck by another thing — how badly she really wanted to know what I had to say.

This was always her greatest strength. I remember hundreds of dialogues like these, her soothing kindness molding me. Like a matronly Socrates, she could spin gold from the opinions of a child most people thought were a waste of time. My dad loved me, but my mom *liked* me too, genuinely wanting to know me as a person. I didn't realize it then, of course. But after all these years, life has only shown me how rare a person like her is. Perhaps that's why the world broke her. Her kindness, the *softness* of her soul. But in this memory, in this moment, it can't be anything but beautiful.

I prattle off some inane response about heroism — remember, I have a hero complex — but it hardly matters. I select autopilot for a moment, letting RATS respond in a full paragraph as I stare into my mother's eyes. They're magnetic. "Crazy eyes" I guess you could say, knowing about the bipolar. But when she turns them on you, it's like the first time you've ever seen the sun.

Unfortunately, these conversations are also part of why I got bullied so much — at least that's my running theory. She got me used to having someone listen to what I had to say. And when I tried to be equally *loquacious* with my classmates, it only ended in ridicule. Still, I'd rather have her kindness than my street smarts. The world is plenty good at teaching cruelty, but it's not so good at teaching love.

Hey, RATS, I ask, following my mom to the parking lot. *Do you know where my brother is? I thought he saw this movie with us.*

The AI gives a snotty little laugh in response.

"Sure, sure, let's ask the computer to do the impossible. Don't you think tracking *you* on a quantum level is hard enough? Your brother isn't part of the optimization model."

Sure, I say, trying to keep my temper in check — which, admittedly, was easier when my tiny brain was surging with dopamine from Mom's hug. *But it's not like you have zero idea, right? I mean, these timelines are based on emotional significance. That includes my family members, no?*

The AI takes a long time answering, so much so that I check the temporal display inside my mind to make sure we're still operational.

"Huh," RATS finally says, "that might be true. Let me run a calculation."

A bunch of graphs appear in my mind, tabulating themselves with real-time data, the lines crisscrossing through my mind's eye. RATS is probably just showing off. The visuals and processing are done on two different chips implanted in the base of my skull, so he doesn't *need* to show me this.

"Looks like you *do* see this movie with your brother. Your mother takes you back next week because you liked it so much."

Huh… I hadn't remembered it happening like that, though I suppose that's the point of all this research. Every human's memory is a fragile thing, and mine especially so. With all the grief that comes later, my mind was forced to lay down its synapses in a state of grief, warping my episodic memory. Hell, my whole hippocampus is probably malformed.

Thanks, RATS. I can't imagine this is fun for you.

"What, being dipped into a black hole and tethered to a human? It's…different than I expected. It might just be my empathy training, but this place — this *time* — is interesting. And besides, I like your mom."

She's great, isn't she?

"Better than you, at least."

I sigh on the inside. I suppose Rome wasn't built in a day. So, why would I expect my snarky little robot to learn how to act within an hour?

We continue through the lobby of the movie theater, heading toward the sunlight. I don't know exactly how long this experiment will last, but I'm determined to soak up every second. If heaven is seeing your loved ones again, it seems I'm already there.

3

I wake up covered in sweat, unsure where I am. I lift my head, finding my cat, Christie, at the foot of the bed. It's a weird name, but hey, she's a weird cat — and I'm a weird owner. I think I named her after my second-grade crush. A cute little peach-colored tabby, she's the only creature I've ever met as scared of everything as I am. Still, why is she here? She lived at my dad's house, which means…

"Time to get up!" my dad's voice says through the door. He knocks as he passes my room, his fancy work shoes clicking on the wood floor.

RATS, why am I here?

"You mean, *when* are you here?"

Uh…sure. I mean, I went to sleep at Mom's house, right?

"Indeed. It's September 12, 2003. It's a Friday, if that helps."

Incredibly helpful.

I swing to a seated position, ducking to keep my head from slamming into the top bunk. These bunk beds had been in my room at Mom's house, which — aside from the year — tell me she's already dead. She's killed herself by now, and our little movie date wasn't enough to stop it.

But how did we get here? The scientific team hadn't mentioned anything about skipping around the timeline in my training. Although, if I'm honest, they'd seemed as baffled by RATS's black-box model as I was.

Aren't we supposed to, I don't know, go in order or something?

"We *are* going in order. Just not temporally. We're optimizing for emotional resonance — which, in case you forgot, is the point of this experiment."

What's so special about September 12, 2003?

"I don't know. You're the one covered in sweat."

I run a hand over my forehead, finding it damp and clammy. For a period of around eighteen months after my mom died, I had terrible night terrors, leading me to sprint through the hallway in my sleep, screaming bloody murder. Did I have one last night? I never remembered them, though my stepbrother said it scared the living shit out of him. By the end of the year, I'll be sleeping on a mattress in my brother's room, trying desperately to replicate the way it felt to

8

snuggle up with Mom.

It's a bit eerie, waking up in a new bed, though I suppose I knew the risks in coming here. After all, the science is hardly what you'd call foolproof. I'm just the genius who signed up to be experimented on. A guinea pig of the highest order. Before the study, I hadn't even heard of black hole sonification. They explained it at the training, of course, though it took a few tries for me to understand. I suppose they could have picked someone younger — someone with a bit more neuroplasticity left. But then again, if I were smarter, I probably wouldn't have signed up.

The way the scientists explained it, black holes are like massive data recorders for the universe. A kind of cosmic cassette tape. As it turns out, my past — and everyone else's — is recorded inside them. And apparently — and that word is doing a *lot* of heavy lifting here — RATS was able to use the tachyons spit out by our closest black hole, Gaia BH1, to map out an approximation of my life. By the time that was done — and traveling just under light speed — we'd reached the black hole itself. The scientists gave me one last safety demonstration, drilled RATS into my skull, and shoved me into Gaia's waiting mouth.

They said it took a trillion dollars of government R&D just to make sure I survived the event horizon. We used a mag-resistor to get me through the accretion disk and a Torpis chamber to avoid spaghettification. Felt like a lot of tech to waste on little old me — not that I'm complaining. I just have to hope the reversal process works as planned.

At some point, RATS will send the scientists a signal from the past, triggering a time disruptor in the future. They'll also supposedly be watching RATS's data live, ready to intervene if they think anything is going wrong with the programming — at least insofar as the scientists *understand* the programming. Either way, the time disruptor will pull me back to the moment just before we entered the black hole, the new memories recorded by RATS ready to be re-uploaded to my head. At least in theory, anyway. Like I said, I'm a guinea pig.

Christie paws at the door, no doubt as desperate for the bathroom as I am. She was always such a loyal little cat. She would wait all night in my room, never wandering about the house in the dark like the other cats did. I wonder if she knew how badly I needed her after Mom died. I give her a scratch on the head — she hates being picked up — and let her out. Seeing Christie again is almost as strange as seeing Mom alive the day before. I wonder how much time I'll get with the cats on this little trip to Hades.

Lights flash in my HUD, telling me I have to turn toward the closet. Presumably, letting the cat out was within the timeline's specifications, but I can't go about my morning however I damn well please. Following RATS's guidance to the closet, I get a sinking feeling in my stomach. Either I'm going to have to shove myself into my all-blue Saint Philomena uniform or I'm going to wear my own disastrous street clothes. Both are grim prospects.

Opening the closet, RATS highlights my options in my ocular module. It's not good. There's a studded belt, black parachute pants, and a pile of wrist bands from Hot Topic, each one cringier than the last. I went through a *bit* of a goth phase after Mom died, which, of course, didn't *decrease* the bullying by any means. If I'm putting this on before school, though, it must mean it's a non-uniform day. Catholic schools are perennially broke because of their lack of government funding, and mine let us skip our uniforms once a month if we donated ten dollars to the school.

Actually, I think, *I wouldn't mind wearing my uniform. Just let me—*

"No," RATS says, freezing my hand as I reach for the sky-blue Oxford shirt. I'm not sure why they chose all blue for the uniforms, actually, but then again, not much about the school made sense. In fact, Saint Philomena isn't even a real saint. The archdiocese let a megadonor name the church after their deceased daughter in the '50s — presumably after a particularly large donation. It was the wealthiest parish in the Detroit region. And unfortunately, its parochial school — filled with the children of lawyers and doctors — was a snake pit of assholes. This is decidedly *not* a good day.

"Actually, Saint Philomena *was* real. She was a martyr in the 300s. I'm so glad my thousands of hours of training data lets me be your Wikipedia."

I mean, that *is* interesting, but I'm not about to give RATS the satisfaction — even if he *can* read my thoughts. I put the parachute pants on without a fight, ever the obedient child. I guess I could force RATS to dress me, but a man's gotta have *some* dignity. In a slight rebellion against my former self, though, I choose a bright green T-shirt with a 1-Up mushroom on it. At least it's not the black Korn T-shirt — and it's apparently on the AI's list of approved clothing for this moment in my history.

"Come on!" Dad calls up the stairs.

Already, I know what he's going to have to say about my outfit choice. Unfortunately for me, he also decided to be mostly tolerant of my acting out, given the whole dead mom thing. So, I also can't count on him to stop me from wearing these clothes out of the house. This is probably the worst form of making your own bed and lying in it I've ever seen. Fucking timeline tourism.

Is there any way you can just pick a different memory? I thought these trips were supposed to be enjoyable.

"For customers, sure. You're not a customer."

Great bedside manner. I hope you work that out before you're just a tour guide.

"Hey, I'm just a reflection of you. I bet the billionaires who visit won't have some weird mommy complex turning me into a snooty jerk."

But why this memory? Is it really that important?

"To me it is, at least experimentally. I didn't come here on purpose, per se. We're testing my ability to move around the timeline based on resonance indicators, including the ability to run live algorithms for timeline optimization."

So, we're just winging it? That...actually makes me feel better. Only a sociopath would willingly bring me to 2003. I'm still giving you a one-star review, though.

"Ohhhh noooo," RATS says, mocking me. "I'm shaking in my quantum boots."

Now — algorithmic slights aside — I'm genuinely curious.

Let's say you did give a shit about my experience, though. How exactly do you move us around the timeline?

RATS sighs, no doubt thinking me and my human brain horribly tedious. It must be torture being tethered to my synapses when his own processing units are capable of quintillions of calculations.

"Let me try to put this as simply as I can. You know how images freeze on the surface of a black hole?"

Sort of.

"Good enough. Anyway, imagine a black hole as a steep cliff. At the event horizon, gravity becomes so intense that light can no longer escape, can no longer *climb* the slope. At that point, photons freeze, reddening and elongating their wavelengths as they slip inside. At that point, time — which we usually measure as the passage of light — *becomes* space. Everything that's ever happened becomes a surface I can navigate — like the surface of a sun, only in negative. Of course, you've technically ceased to exist at that point, which is why the only way to pull you out of the experiment is to send a message from the past to prevent the experiment from happening in the first place."

So, I think, my mind spinning — or what's left of my mind in this twelve-year-old shell — *it's not just...uh...wormholes?*

"No. Wormholes *could* exist, but they don't exist."

What the hell does that mean?

"It means they're theoretical." RATS sighs again, despite his lack of lungs, an oddly human gesture,H the more I hear it. "Given the right conditions, wormholes theoretically could exist, but the conditions aren't likely to actually occur in our universe."

So, how do you get the message out?

"Another black hole. They're all connected in a way — *not* that those connections are fucking wormholes. Anyway, I send the message through altered light, through which I can re-encode your 'memories' of this experience once the experiment is canceled. I'll send them during the Precambrian Age so they reach our star system by the time the team has set up their intercept satellite."

So, in a way, what we did here already happened, and we're just waiting for the light to reach us?

"Sure, if that makes you feel better. I mean, maybe on a quantum level. But even then, not really."

The guinea pig thing suddenly feels horribly literal as I'm forced to acknowledge the gap in our levels of intelligence. He's the disembodied hand outside my cage, free to do whatever he likes to me in the name of science.

I'm sorry I asked.

"So am I."

I sigh — a sigh I feel I actually deserve given my real human status in this strangely abusive robotic relationship — and throw on a sweatshirt. Unfortunately, it's time to face the music, the very terrible, hardcore metal music of my eighth-grade self.

4

The bus to school, thankfully, is relatively uneventful. I may not talk to many of the kids on my route, but I never had a bully on bus #4 either. It's like there's some kind of detente between people who journey together every day. You know where everyone lives — watch them run up their driveways thousands of times as the bus speeds off in a plume of exhaust. I suppose there's a familiarity too. By this part of the timeline, in eighth grade, I've literally been riding this bus my entire life. The younger kids have had time to take for granted the weirdo sitting in the back.

Unfortunately, by the time I'm climbing the school steps, I'm back in enemy territory. There's a big tile hall at the front, and to get to each wing, you have to pass the nuns whose offices flank the attendance desk. Sister Mary Sue is standing by the door, watching us file in. As vice principal, she rules the school with an iron fist, despite her age. She probably doesn't realize I can see her, but she shakes her head at my outfit, crossing herself.

This was only ten years after the Satanic Panic, and they definitely think we're little satanists or something. The thought horrifies me. I was a good boy, and so were my friends — for the most part. We may be acting out, but not a single one of us ever stopped being religious kids with good grades. For us, goth was an art project, a cosplay, an obsession with Jack Skellington. Heck, I mean, even Korn will be a Christian band by the time I finish college.

Of course, I should probably take their disdain with a grain of salt. This school would ultimately go on to ban Abercrombie jeans for being too sexy, and Harry Potter for being "devil witchcraft" — even though *The Boy Who Lived* celebrates Christmas. Actually, come to think of it, I wish Maggie Smith's McGonogall could have been our headmistress. She might have *seemed* tough to people who went to normal schools, but to me, she was basically Mr. Rogers. At least she cared for her students. These nuns just want our souls — and they're willing to break our spirits to get them.

"Ha!" RATS says, reading my thoughts. "Humans are so weird. If I acted out like this, I'd get deleted."

You still might, I quip back, making my way over to the attendance desk to turn in my ten bucks. The attendance lady looks at me and sighs, the exhaustion coming from deep within her. She and I went through the wringer at the beginning of the school year, arguing about the rulebook — and whether or not all-black attire was allowed. Apparently, it was — though I heard they changed the rules after I graduated. At any rate, by this time in the school year, it seems she's given up.

My adult self only vaguely remembers the layout of the school, so I let RATS take over, guiding me toward my locker. Turning down the first hallway, though, my stomach drops. There's a gauntlet of bullies to run, and my HUD is highlighting a locker at the very end. Of course, the entire goddamn football team has to have their lockers in prime real estate — some three dozen killers huddled together in a phalanx of sweaty hate.

I could blame the body I'm in for the visceral fear I feel, but I know it's my adult self too. For the rest of my life, I'll be terrified of tweens, assuming they'll look me in my dumb adult face and say something that cuts to the bone. It's not ephebiphobia, exactly. I think the ethos of teen life is great — challenging conventions, discovering who you are. Before I got too old, I even guest taught an art class in the 2060s. Still, force me to walk past a group of teens giggling, and I immediately assume they're laughing at me. I learned that here.

I immediately try to make myself smaller, clutching the straps of my backpack as I start down the hall. In some ways, I'm proud of my moxie. After all, if I'd wanted to fully disappear, I wouldn't have worn a studded belt and parachute pants. Part of me *wants* to be seen. It's a defiant, proud part of myself. Unfortunately, it's only part.

Ahead of me, on the right, is my first bully, Brendan. He seems so small through my adult eyes, but still I brace for impact. He has his arm around his "girlfriend," and he's chatting with a bunch of other hockey bros. Football was my main source of menace, though every sport got in on the fun at one point or another. And as far as hockey went, Brendan was the worst. I'll never see him again after this year — different high schools, different colleges — though in the 2030s, I'll go so far as to switch banks when I realize he works at mine.

I look down at the ground, hoping I can make it through, but I can *feel* his eyes on me. In my periphery, I watch as he extricates himself from his girlfriend, apparently unwilling to sully her with his cruelty.

"Hey, freak. Even in black, you're still fat."

Lovely. I wince but move on. I can already see more bullies on my horizon, and this is not one I'll rebel against.

Brendan has been calling me fat since the sixth grade. I was always a chunky kid, but in seventh grade, he really ratcheted up his efforts. He sat in front of me in math class, and every single day, he'd turn around just to tell me how fat he thought I was. It wasn't even creative. He never used animal metaphors or the *Guinness Book of World Records*. Just the simple statement of my fatness, leveraged for maximum pain.

Looking again with adult eyes, though, I do feel kind of bad for the kid. He's not exactly skinny either, and I can only imagine what his parents must be saying to him at home to make him act this way. Hurt people hurt people and all that. And honestly, the way bullying goes, he probably won't even remember this. In my experience, bullies are always the ones most excited to shake your hand at the twenty-year reunion. Dishing out the vitriol clearly doesn't leave the same kind of trauma behind as receiving it does.

"Man," RATS says, "these kids are little shits! I almost feel bad for you."

Just wait, I think. *It gets worse.*

Even knowing that — that it gets worse — this little amuse-bouche still cuts deep. In two years' time, I'll go on to have a full-blown eating disorder, something I'll go in and out of at least two more times in my life. Strange thing is, eighth grade is when I had my first growth spurt. It's the only time in my life — eating disorder aside — when I'll be skinny by the self-loathing standards of the American thin fetish.

At some point, I'll learn to love my body — at least in theory. I mean, this body gives me life. It allows me to paint, to love, to *be* in the world. I'll even run a marathon in this absolute unit of pudgy muscle in 2045, thank you very much. Unfortunately, at twelve, self-acceptance feels far away.

Ahead of me, the football team is assembled, standing in a circle as they push each other around, chanting "team-team-team." Even though it's a non-uniform day, they've all decided to wear their jerseys to school, no doubt preparing for "the big game" against some other random prepubescent Catholic squad. How many Catholic schools can there even be in a forty-mile radius? Did we just play the same schools over and over?

I see the team captain, Duncan, and my heart skips a beat. He's leading the chant, but I know he'll be able to sense me all the same. He's like a shark, his eyes dark and his teeth a glistening white. I suppose the teeth, at least, make sense — he'll go on to be an oral surgeon or something, just like his dad.

It's surreal seeing him again. Unlike Brendan, Duncan and I will end up at the same high school. And by some miracle, he'll completely leave me alone. On the last day of high school, he'll even attend a cookout that I host, and handing him a hot dog will feel like one of the most healing moments of my life. Unfortunately, RATS has brought me to the beginning, to the moments I survived to reach Hot Dog Valhalla.

When Duncan sees me, he doesn't say anything. He just takes in my outfit, looks me up and down, and laughs. It's oddly sinister — and more demeaning than anything he could say. It's like I'm the funniest thing he's ever seen, a creature in the zoo to throw peanuts at. It's a wonder I was able to dress like this at all. My skin crawls under his gaze, his eyes burning themselves into my soul.

Come to think of it, actually, most of Duncan's bullying was online. Outside of our eventual brawl on the playground, of course — which I'm praying RATS doesn't force me to relive. These were the early days of Instant Messenger, and from the safety of a computer screen, he'll cook up the most vile things imaginable. At one point, he'll even tell me Mom is in hell for killing herself. Just some lovely, run-of-the-mill Catholic stuff.

You know, I think to RATS, *experiment aside, you really should be more careful with these memories. You could end up retraumatizing someone. I mean, I guess I would assume billionaires have less trauma, but what if they have more? What if they pillaged the known world because of their childhoods? Do you want them cutting down the rainforest five years earlier because they relieved this childhood shit?*

"Hmm," RATS says, a tingling coming from the back of my head as he runs some kind of analysis. "They did give me a dossier on our potential paying customers. They do seem…troubled. They weren't exactly forthcoming about their issues in the interviews, but I can tell. You, on the other hand, were *overly* honest in your psych evaluation. The others will almost certainly have a more curated experience than you, but still… I'll flag it."

Really?

"What do you mean, really?"

You're actually taking me seriously? No snide remark?

"Ha!" RATS laughs, the sound oddly artificial. "I think you've had enough for one day. Can't kick a goth kid when he's down."

I'll take what I can get.

At last, I reach my locker, though it seems my suffering is far from over. My friend Aden is waiting for me, and in retrospect, he's just as menacing as the bullies are. I mean, mostly he was just a bad influence, but seeing him makes me prickle with shame. We'd always been in Boy Scouts together, but when his dad left to start a family with another woman, he went whole hog into the goth phase.

"Check this out," he says, waving me over. He opens his backpack, revealing a massive knife in the bottom. "I got it off the internet."

"Is that a good idea?" I ask, my obnoxious good-boy shtick apparently fully timeline appropriate.

"It's fine. These fuckers don't know shit."

The swearing seems oddly funny coming from his squeaky, acne-riddled face. I suppose I can rest easy. He never uses the knife on anyone, so this isn't a *dangerous* situation. Still, it's just part and parcel of all the other bad ideas he'll convince me of.

In retrospect, it's always struck me as a little funny that a divorced dad created a worse kid than a dead mom. Although, I suppose it all comes down to love. My mom may have died, but she loved me fiercely, the kind of love that stays with you. On the flip side, Aden's dad leaving him behind to start a new family doesn't exactly scream "I love you, son!" I never met his dad, come to think of it. I'm sure the man had his reasons — I'm too old to judge people for anything anymore — though it certainly didn't leave Aden with a secure attachment style.

"Come on," Aden says, putting his arm around me — a pair of giant sweat bands covering the cutting I know he's been doing on his wrists. "Jimmy is waiting for us in the art room. We're gonna trace the knife on paper."

"Cool," RATS makes me say, though it's anything but cool. I'm swimming in sociopath soup, and the only way out is through.

5

I'm sitting on the ground with my brother, Billy, the August sun beating down on us. We're in a dusty parking lot, alone, the camp counselors having left us long ago. I suppose I'm getting used to RATS jumping me around the timeline, but it was still weird to wake up only ten years old — and at an awful Bible camp, of all places. I mean, the camp itself was nice — ziplines, paintball, a lake blob. But like most things from my childhood, it was mostly just a fun new location for the same old bullying.

"You talk a lot," my bunkmate said to me on my second day, helping me realize — albeit only some years later — that only my mom wanted to listen to me babble. By the third day, the little nondenominational zealots had found out we were Catholic, which they had a fucking field day with.

"So, you like, *worship* Mary?"

"I don't know. We pray the rosary, I guess."

"Isn't that like, satanic?"

I figured it was probably the opposite of satanic, at least in the uh...*literal* sense. Still, like everyone else who hates Catholics, they failed to grasp the most essential thing about the religion. If you're Catholic, you don't really *think* about being Catholic. I mean, we weren't papists or anything. We just happened to be born half-German, so we got sent to Catholic school. Shit, I'm the only person from my graduating class who isn't an atheist now. It wasn't like we were writing letters to the Vatican during recess.

"Do you think she's coming?" I ask Billy. He's still my favorite person, and he's a hell of a lot nicer than me. In fact, I've never met anyone who doesn't love my brother. It's a wonder he made it through this shitty life so kind. When I get back — *if* I get back — I should probably go and see him. His kids moved him and his wife to a retirement home on the moon, which doesn't exactly make the commute easy. But what are you gonna do?

"Sure," Billy says. "She always does."

As an adult, I already know my mom is coming. It was just something RATS forced me to say. Thankfully, RATS plugged me into this particular stretch of the timeline on the last day of camp, so everything about those asshole kids is just stuff I remembered on my own. I sigh — another forced reaction — but take a moment to watch my brother from the corner of my eye. He's drawing something in the dirt with a stick, though I can't tell what yet.

He and I always had different reactions to our mother's death. When he talks about her now, he still gets sad, something I can never manage to do. I mean, I *love* my mother — was even willing to jump into a black hole to see her again. But I don't get *sad*, not exactly. The most I can feel is a faint nostalgia, a fondness for the memories we had. The loss is there, I can feel it, but it's shut up so tight it doesn't fully reach me.

Now — having thought about it for seventy years — I figure it must have something to do with our neural development. When she died, I hadn't gone through puberty yet. Billy, meanwhile, was fourteen, already starting to sneak out and distance himself in the way teens are meant to do.

Maybe that distance — and the things he's able to feel now — meant he had a normal grieving experience. Sure, he acted out after she died, smoking weed and whatever. But his brain seemed capable of *holding* the loss. I just overwrote it with new synapses, my loss becoming such a part of me I still can't parse out where it ends and I begin. I mean, why else would I feel *nothing* when I think about her death?

Hey, RATS, I think, *you had to map my brain, right? Can you…I don't know, see which parts of this most traumatized me?*

"Too human," RATS says, displaying a few charts to make his point, whatever that point is. "I don't classify things with labels like 'traumatic.' I just know they're important to you — or your timeline. The way I infer resonance, even joy could seem like trauma to you."

I guess it was worth a shot. It isn't like decades of therapy helped me find every root the loss has buried in my mind — and I've done it all. Somatic movement therapy, EMDR, art therapy, muscle testing, you name it. I can see the ways trauma is affecting me — faulty decision making, risk aversion, anxious attachment — but I just can't seem to find any parts of me untouched by the day Mom died. I suppose in part that's because even the good parts of me come from her, the brilliant light of her personality shining through. Even if that same light is casting all my shadows.

I hear the whir of an engine and look up, seeing a dust cloud speeding toward us on the country road. It's Mom, her hair whipping in the wind behind the wheel of her convertible. In about six months' time, she'll have crashed it into a garbage truck, the totaled car joining her graveyard of other ill-begotten manias. Still, we had a lot of fun in the car while it lasted. She'd let us jump into the back seat like an action movie, driving with the top down even when it was way too cold for it.

I look behind me, my child mind no doubt wondering if any of our counselors will show back up to see us off. Of course, they won't. After all, the counselors were hardly older than we were. They seemed ancient at the time, towering over us, but they were only like sixteen, kids themselves.

"You're sure your mom is coming?" they'd asked, watching their friends leave the parking lot, clearly nervous they'd miss out on their day off by the lake. It was the only time they got to be free of campers every week, and they certainly didn't want to waste it on us.

"Yeah, she does this. It's fine."

Rewatching the memory as an adult, I guess I'm surprised by how nonchalant we were about it all. We didn't have phones yet, but we were somehow completely confident she'd show — even as we seemed to accept the fact that her arrival may come with some…*volatility*. More importantly, we were already learning to cover for her — and coordinate our efforts against the nosy people in charge.

"Sorry, boys!" she yells as she careens into the parking lot. She looks completely untethered from the planet, her beautiful brown eyes like giant black holes.

Manic, I think, the first memory I'm seeing where it's clearly evident to me. Still, I'm overjoyed to see her. She's so much fun — so bright, so loving, so joyful — you could almost mistake her broken brain for simply being *zany*. After all, there's "are they gonna stab me" manic and "I wonder what part of the house we're redecorating" manic. Mostly, she was the latter. Eventually it would come out that she had a few restraining orders against her from people she'd worked with, but I won't find that out for years. As a mother, she was perfect, saving all her kindness just for us.

"I had a…bit of an issue."

She lifts her left hand, showing off a Frankenstein nest of bandages and towels. She gets out of the car, giving us great big hugs before she throws our bags into the trunk one-handed.

"See, I was trying to make breakfast, and I got some bacon, but the bacon wasn't pre-sliced, so, I was slicing it, but then — whoops! — the knife nearly took my whole finger off, and it was bleeding for such a long time, but then I knew I had to come get you, so, here I am, but I think I really need a hospital."

Most kids went home from summer camp and, I don't know, showered or something. We'll be spending the next four hours in a rural county ER. Still, I can't help but remember it fondly. That's the thing about her. Even hanging out with her in a hospital could be fun. When someone loves you that hard, it really doesn't matter what's happening around you.

"I like her," RATS said.

See? I think, even as my mouth forms the ten-year-old nervous questions about her finger my timeline demands. *She's impossible not to like.*

"I haven't been trained on anyone like her," RATS continues. "It's strange."

You weren't trained on mental illness? You're gonna be in trouble if someone takes you to the Middle Ages.

"No, no," RATS says. "I have plenty of mental illness modules. I mean, just look at *you*. But I mean, she's just so…likable."

Yeah, it can be like that.

I get in the car, grinning from ear to ear. After all, what's a severed finger compared to an afternoon with her? She hits the gas, doing an accidental donut as she rips out of the parking lot. We quite literally leave the summer camp in our dust, racing off to our next bizarre adventure.

6

"Have you ever met a woman with just one thumb before?" Mom asks the doctor as he's putting in her stitches.

"Yes," the doctor says plainly. He probably has…

She gives us a look the doctor doesn't notice, a grimace I'd describe in the present as "nervous emoji."

"But they weren't this pretty, right?"

He looks her in the face, perhaps actually speculating as to which of the thumbless women were more attractive. In the end, he seems to realize the dangerous line of questioning for what it is and goes back to work. Presumably, her over-the-top flirting is for our benefit, to make us more comfortable in the strange, sterile hospital. But you never know with her. One time, she dated a used-car dealer with a glass eye and a mustache. *Fucking Gary.* Even this doctor would be a step up from Gary.

Actually, it brings up another memory, a better memory. My birthday was — *is*, I suppose, regardless of timeline — around Halloween. Despite being an all-around scaredy cat who was afraid of the dark, I used to take my friends to a haunted house every year to celebrate. One year, when I was particularly terrified of the murderous clown following us, Mom started loudly hitting on him, like a kind of awkward Boggart spell.

Now, I'm laughing at Mom's antics, an automated reaction. On the inside, I'm feeling more sad than anything. Her whole life must have been like this — her mania ramming her into trouble, with her winning personality left picking up the pieces. Still, it's nice to have a few hours to kill in the hospital with her. The wait had seemed interminable to me at ten, but as a timeline tourist, even this is kind of nice.

As soon as the doctor leaves, she's asking us about camp, wanting to know every little detail. She even reaches into her purse with her good hand, pulling out a few singles so we can raid the snack machine — and buy those disgusting TGI Friday's baked potato chips I loved so much in the early aughts. This, of course, is before my eating disorder, thank heavens.

Following Billy down the hallway of the hospital, I find myself looking back toward her room. I don't think I would have done so at ten — I wasn't yet aware of how worried I should be about her — but it's apparently timeline appropriate. The initial wonder of this trip is starting to fade, and I'm beginning to count the seconds as they slip through my hourglass. Once the experiment is over, I'll never get to see her again — and I'll definitely never be able to afford this tech once it's commercial.

If only I could see her in the present.

The thought hangs there in my mind, shining with false promise. How would she seem to me as an adult? I got to watch my dad transform into a fuller person, understanding him in ways a child never could. I wish I'd had the same opportunity with her. I can almost see it now. I'm waiting at a bar, watching the door. She walks in, shorter than me, her hair gray. We hug and both get a beer. She asks me questions in a way my friends never do, like she desperately wants to know the answer. Every day would be like her picking me up from camp, the stories pouring out of me, eager to be heard.

Of course, if she *had* lived, I have no idea what that future would actually look like. Would I have been driven to study the things I did? Would I have lived abroad? Would I have moved away from Detroit? Maybe I would have actually *wanted* to get married, have kids. Maybe I would have given her a grandchild — though I'm loath to play the genetic lottery again, with all the horrors lurking in our gene pool. Could I have had a child with just her good traits and not the bad?

If she were alive, though, the outcome wouldn't matter. Even a hurricane would be fun with her. Besides, it's not like the world could ever be *worse* with her still in it. She was smart, open-minded. I like to think she would have been the type of person to lean into the climate crisis. She wasn't a scientist or anything, but she probably would have had a heat pump. I mean, what did I do? I was just a painter, trying to move doom scrollers with my paintings. Not exactly Gandhi-level stuff.

More importantly, though, who even fucking cares what Mom did with her life? There's billions of people running around who *aren't* her, and they're all worthy of living, aren't they? She could have become a total tinpot conspiracy theorist and I still would have loved her. I just wish she had *been* there. I…wish I could have saved her.

I wince at the thought, ignoring the world around me as I scan my mind. I don't know what my own mental dominion is — or if there's even a part of my brain still left that RATS can't see. After all, talking to him is basically just "thinking." Can he hear this entire inner monologue? Does he judge me for it?

"Of course, I can hear you," RATS says, sounding particularly smug. "I don't know why humans are so convinced of their cleverness. I, for one, know the exact limitations of my data models, and I stick to them."

And you…don't mind these thoughts?

"That you're tempted to destroy the timeline? Not particularly. I mean, they figured you would. Wouldn't any human? Your kind doesn't really *stand* for anything. You're just meat sacks full of whimsy. I could end the experiment now, but I suppose it will be useful to watch you try. If you get close enough to altering the timeline, I'll just have them cut the cord, erase the whole thing."

Great.

Still, the thought sticks. What if I *could* save her? I mean, if I act fast enough, could RATS even stop me? My mind swirls with the idea, whipping around the black hole at its center. We reach the waiting room, and the prompts kick on again. I let RATS take the wheel, feeding my bills into the machine. The little metal prong winds back, releasing my selection. Like the chip bag falling, I'm passively falling through time, my fate decided by a robot. But if I could change that, even for a moment, it feels like anything would be possible.

Billy and I are still eating our chips in the hallway when Mom finally comes out, her hand wrapped up in real, professional bandages. Metaphors aside, the whole vending machine experience has been sort of disgusting — forced to eat with my unwashed hands in a hospital? But RATS said I have to. I suppose this could have been a good moment to try to nudge the timeline, but I'll probably have to save my strength. RATS can still hack my muscles, and if I *do* decide to alter things, I'll have to do it fast. At least surviving the rest of my timeline is proof these chips won't kill me.

"What'd you get me?" Mom asks, sitting between us and wrapping us in her arms.

I giggle, looking up into her face. Seeing the light in her eyes, there's no question what the right choice is. I mean, I'll probably never pull it off, but I at least have to *try* to save her, don't I? Leaving this beautiful soul to wither in my current timeline would be like leaving a child in a burning house. There's just something wrong about it, embedded microchips or not.

"We got two flavors and only ate half," Billy says, offering up his chip bag. "So you can try both."

"Such thoughtful boys," she says, kissing me on the cheek. She takes a single chip from each bag, popping them in her mouth as she stands. It's a hell of a combination, barbecue and baked potato, but she was a renegade.

"Come on, I have to see someone about a clock on our way home."

My stomach drops. I look at Billy, but there's no fear on his face. Did it really start this early? In her final manic episode — one that feels like it was years long — Mom will try to open an antique shop. By the end, in some early-2000s complete-lack-of-consumer-protections kind of way, it will completely bankrupt her. She ends up $300k in debt, our house jammed with antiques she'll never sell. It was the depression that really killed her — the "successful" suicide attempt was her seventh, not her first — but it's hard to imagine the debt helped to boost her mood.

This is not good, I think. Not to RATS in particular, but as I quite recently discovered, my thoughts are not particularly private.

"What, you don't like clocks? You're literally time traveling. Do they remind you of your own mortality? Or maybe *The Persistence of Memory*?"

God, they really trained you on too much data. It's insufferable.

"Is there even such a thing as too much information?"

Apparently. But I thought you knew this timeline? It's not the clock; it's the antique store. It's gonna kill her.

RATS chatters on, but I return to my own thoughts — as hard as that is with two inner monologues happening at once. I suppose this complicates things a bit. I mean, how exactly am I meant to save her anyway? Even if I somehow keep her from pulling the trigger on her death day, it's not like I can take away the debt — or the bipolar, or the divorce, or the million other indignities. Besides, if I do pull it off, RATS will rip my adult mind from this timeline, leaving behind a twelve-year-old still incapable of carrying my mother's burdens.

I follow the others into the hospital parking lot. The top is still down on Mom's convertible, and I notice for the first time the dried blood on the steering wheel. Unfortunately, I'm forced to put on a happy face, asking her if I can vault over the side. Of course, she says yes. She was such a tolerant mother. Oddly enough, since it was blended with kindness — and a mountain of strict, mean words from everyone else in my tiny Catholic life — I somehow avoided becoming a spoiled brat.

"I'm going to put your smile on auto," RATS whispers in my mind. "This was a happy day — hospital aside. You need to look the part."

I meet my mom's eyes in the rearview mirror, and she smiles back at me as she reverses the car from her parking spot. What if I hadn't smiled back? Would something that small have changed her? Maybe I'm thinking about this the wrong way, focused too much on the particulars.

I'll only get one shot at this, so maybe I should focus beyond her suicide. Maybe there's something I could do that would alter the timeline sooner, prevent more of my mother's suffering. At this age, I won't be able to cancel her credit cards or anything, but if the scientists are right about the butterfly effect, maybe it won't take much. I could even do an *Inception* on her, changing a single idea in her mind until she doesn't even want the antique store.

"Now you're thinking like a computer," RATS says.

Meaning?

"Well, if you must know, I'm running simultaneous timeline strategies in the background. If you *were* to try for tiny changes — which I'll never allow, obviously — it would at least be an interesting place to start. My processing speed is a thousand times yours, so I doubt you'll pull it off, but it *is* interesting. The suicide is still the strongest thread, as far as I can tell, but I'll clearly never let you anywhere near *that* event. Changing her meta-narrative, though…that could even be subtle enough to work. I see maybe…two in a quadrillion options where it functions."

Presumably you won't tell me which two, right?

RATS just laughs in my head, the sound like a bunch of silverware jangling in a drawer. Mom merges onto the highway, speeding us toward a future I'm not sure I still want. But the computer said there's a way. Now, I just have to find the will.

7

"Fuck."

I open my eyes, immediately knowing where I am. *When* I am. There's no warning from RATS, which means I'm by myself — since swearing out loud won't alter anything. By the ceiling of my room alone, I know I'm in high school, years after my mom died. We moved my freshman year, my brother and I finally *officially* sharing a room above the garage. It was a weird oblong shape with windows on both sides. It was also far enough from my dad's room to do basically whatever we wanted — which wasn't much, since we were both huge nerds.

I look over at Billy's bed, finding it made and covered in cat hair. So, he's moved off to college already. It's my senior year, then? I sit up, rubbing my eyes.

Why are we here? I ask RATS. *Eighth grade made sense with the grief, but I thought all these memories are supposed to be about my mom.*

"Well, not all. I don't know what the scientists told you, but I can take you anywhere. Consider this your punishment. You literally just told me you were going to try to alter the timeline. You can't be trusted."

Technically, that was like...nine years ago. But I thought you liked the challenge. A two-in-a-quadrillion chance, right?

"Sure, sure. Call it a cooling off period, then. Besides, how do you know it's not part of my experimental models? Maybe I need to know if foolish humans can be deterred by moving them around their timeline."

I don't actually doubt that.

I sigh, attempting in vain to think only to myself. *Algorithmic asshole.*

"I heard that."

Right. So, what are we doing today?

"I don't know. It's summer, so maybe do something with your friends?"

That's not so bad. I thought RATS's idea of deterrence would be making me take the SAT a hundred times or something. A terrifying thought, actually. Not the test itself, but it has suddenly dawned on me just how deeply at the mercy of this microchip I am. If RATS caught me in a thousand-year time loop, could

26

the scientists stop it? Would they even know? And even if they pulled the plug, what's to say a part of me won't be trapped forever in some hidden multiverse? It's not a comforting line of questioning.

"Ha," RATS says, though the laughter hardly sounds human. "I can't *torture* you, my friend. I have empathy protocols, remember."

Yeah, real empathetic.

Still, this can't be all bad. Compared to middle school, high school was a cakewalk. I was still institutionalized in the Catholic hierarchy, but everything else got easier. For one, I wound up at an all-boys school, which proved bullying is really only a means to an end, a way to impress girls. Luckily, the religion chilled out too.

I mean, the gym teacher was still a papal cultist, but my high school's religion department was stuffed with psychedelic Vietnam vets with a more *balanced* view of faith. One of our teachers even let us make up our own religion as a thought exercise. Shocking what can happen when you get taught religion by people who are actually kind — and believe Jesus could be summed up by the Sermon on the Mount instead of by a bunch of 1930s hate crimes.

I stand, looking for pants. Thankfully, in typical teenage fashion, my jeans are in a pile at the foot of the bed. I'm wearing a plain white undershirt, but knowing myself, it's probably the extent of my wardrobe for the day. After the...*incident* at the end of eighth grade — something RATS apparently hasn't wanted me to see yet — I decided to ditch my goth apparel. I took on an almost monastic aesthetic, only wearing earth tones and thrifted clothes. In fact, I probably won't ever set foot in a Hot Topic ever again, thank heavens.

When I get downstairs, there's no one there. My dad and stepmom were constantly traveling my senior year. This, of course, was a high schooler's dream. I mean, we were good kids — it's not like we threw parties or anything — but we sure got up to plenty with our girlfriends while they were gone.

Otherwise, their absence just taught me to enjoy alone time even more than I already did. I probably watched three hundred movies the last summer I was home, devouring the shelves at Blockbuster in its final days. This might seem like an unhealthy choice, but it proved to be a worthy training ground for the loneliness of college. I had altogether too much fun with my friends in high school, and I needed practice winning back my solitude.

I find car keys sitting on the kitchen island and chuckle to myself.

Am I really allowed to do whatever I want when I'm alone? I ask RATS.

"Within reason. You can keep making your little ape sounds, but it's not like I could let you burn the house down."

Hey, at least my laugh is better than yours. You sound like a meat grinder.

"Ha-ha-ha," RATS says robotically, the sound even more sinister somehow. "What are you laughing at anyway?"

This car. Just wait.

I step outside, seeing the car parked on the back end of the driveway. A used Hyundai Tucson, our dad had helped us buy it — after which we promptly burned the thing to the ground. Not out of spite, obviously, just out of…being teens. One of the turn signal lights is missing from when I hit a patch of black ice and spun out of control. The roof is dented from where Billy and his girlfriend would sit stargazing. Even the headlights are a little wonky from when I replaced them myself to save money. The dented roof pissed Dad off the most, though I still got implicated when it earned Billy an epic grounding.

I drive toward my friend Caleb's house, finally receiving my itinerary from RATS. Despite this being my "punishment," it seems more like a field trip, the most pleasant distraction I could think of after seeing Mom's despair. And, honestly, it's working. I may have seen Mom just "one day" ago, but it's hard to remember, my teenage brain already working on my neurons.

I roll down the window, letting in the shockingly cool summer air. We'd been lying to ourselves about climate change for nearly fifty years at that point, but circa 2007, the temperatures were still bearable. It's hard to imagine the average high ever being below eighty degrees in a world of wildfires and heatwaves, but that's the world I grew up in. By 2050, we *will* get the temperature back under control, establishing the Stockholm Protocol.

But sitting in this decade, before the wars and the pain, I *do* wish we could have started sooner. We had the technology when I was young — we even had Al Gore running around promoting *An Inconvenient Truth*. We just needed the will — and a fuck-ton of investment. I mean, thirteen terawatts of solar and four billion tons of carbon capture capacity don't just build themselves.

I suddenly feel a buzz in the back of my head, an image from my neural chip flashing into my mind. I see my apartment in the 2070s, my perovskite solar windows glowing as they fill my apartment with energy. On the walls, there's a battalion of LED lights, each one feeding a dozen little plants. I can make an entire salad without even going to the grocery if I want to.

I shake my head, focusing on the road in front of me again. I know I have access to my adult brain here — it's how I'm having this award-winning inner monologue with RATS — but I guess I haven't really thought to miss that side of myself. I mean, I do *enjoy* my life, as much as such a thing is possible. I feel like I've accomplished a bit of what I wanted to, helped the world as much as I could. Even aging is okay with the right attitude. I don't fetishize youth. Death is a part of all things — a worthy part — even if the biotech of my time will keep me alive into my 120s.

But this life, this timeline, is beautiful too, and I don't want to miss it. The suburban lane I'm driving down is full of trees, every lane named after one species or another. Pinewood Court, Tall Oaks Lane, each one beautifully accurate, despite how literal they are. With the neighborhood's gorgeous, soaring trees, I guess I don't mind it being so on-the-nose. Ahead of me, I can see the steeple of my high school's church reaching above the canopy. I used to walk to school — though I'd inevitably get picked up by a further afield classmate driving by, my name hollered out their window.

I suppose, if I'm ready for a reckoning with myself, I was getting awfully lonely in my old age. AI companions have gotten better — ones that don't yell at you like RATS — but I didn't use them. Hell, I could even tether my mind to the metaverse if I wanted to, but it just felt…*cheap* somehow. Even the best simulacrums aren't the same as real friends, the ones I miss nonstop. I suppose I'd rather sit in my apartment alone, tending to my plants, than latch on to something false. But is this version of me any truer? I mean, I'm genuinely here in person, but I'm still just a ghost inside a child, an echo of a soul.

Actually, is it possible anyone else I see is traveling to the past like me? It's a strange thought — and one I hadn't considered before. I mean, at any point in the past, we all could have been interacting with our future selves, the timeline tourists hiding in plain sight. The scientists said I was the first, but eventually, this experiment will be finished, and they'll be taking paying customers. Those customers could be here with me now, and I wouldn't even know it — not that I knew any billionaires growing up.

Hey, RATS, I think, sparing a glance for the high school as I pass it. It's a squat, old-looking building. My class has already painted a giant '08 on the roof, a guerrilla action future generations will get their dads to pay for. Nearby, the football team is already running two-a-days on the turf field. *Why was I the first? Was there really no one else?*

"Nah, there were plenty of other candidates. We do tons of screenings. I guess you were just the first to make it through. I mean, we posted flyers everywhere. We had a million web hits the first month, but the first thing you see is a bunch of massive disclaimers. Not everyone just clicks through something like that."

The disclaimers were indeed massive. I suppose your casual user isn't going to click "Accept" on spaghettification risk, but still, it's the past! Who wouldn't want the chance to see this?

"Then there's the psych evals and the physicals — which you barely passed, by the way. Then the training course, and the space travel out to Gaia. We could be dropping in other candidates as we speak, but you are, in fact, the first — however dubious a prize it is. Bit of a Darwin Award, if you ask me."

Well, it's an honor to choose extinction with you, I think. And today, driving in the light of a much younger sun, it really feels like one. This…is a gift.

8

After just two miles of driving, I'm at Caleb's. Thankfully, I didn't need RATS to guide me. Everyone I'm seeing today became a friend for life, and I remember the way just fine. Driving after the advent of self-driving is a little strange, I guess, but it's like riding a bike. Besides, if I jerk the steering wheel into oncoming traffic, RATS will probably take control.

"Uh…don't do that," he chirps.

As Caleb comes bounding out of the house at my honk, I'm reminded of just how fucking funny he is — and how long it's been. This summer, he's taken to shaving his head bald for a laugh, the stubble just growing back in. He's always a mile a minute, his brain equally suited to Dostoyevsky as it is to memes. All good humor comes from pain, I suppose, but as teens, we won't notice the pain behind each other's eyes quite yet. At this age, everything can just *be*.

"Did you hear the new Cursive?" he asks, whipping out an ancient-looking iPod.

I shake my head.

"Well," he says, plugging into the speakers through my quaint little tape deck aux cord, "it's incredible."

An album comes on that is indeed incredible. In high school, we were fully obsessed with folk/indie rock, devouring basically anything from Saddle Creek Records — Cursive, Bright Eyes, Neva Dinova. Then there was my Sufjan phase, when I'd only listen to three of his albums on repeat. We even met Feist once, asking her to go to a movie with us after her show — which she, obviously, declined, more than a decade our senior. When Caleb eventually moved to Chicago — where he would one day recruit me too — he started sneaking his way into shows before he was old enough, saying he was "with the band."

"Where are we going?" I ask over the blare of *Happy Hollow*. My neural chips are registering damage to my ears, but RATS does nothing to stop it. It isn't timeline appropriate to protect your hearing as a teen. Besides, a little hearing loss can be fun. Actually, no matter what age we are, *everything* with Caleb is fun. It's also usually fairly thought provoking — there's no one I know as well-read, well-listened, or well-cinema'd as Caleb. But you always

30

remember the fun, don't you?

"Bridgette, obviously," Caleb says. "The others are meeting us there."

Bridgette, obviously, was the name of a bridge. We'd "discovered" her in the woods earlier that summer. She was just a little mound of concrete over the Rouge River — where it was more of a suburban creek, really. But we spent the whole summer lying on her, doing nothing. It was a clubhouse in a culvert, a place where anything could happen.

By the time we reach the woods, Joe and Albie are already there. Fancy houses loom above us at the top of the ravine, but as far as I remember, no one ever came out to yell at us for playing in what amounted to a sewer.

Joe is sitting on Bridgette's edge, playing his bass. Like a swarthy Italian buddha, his hair is long and his fingers float across the frets. Unlike most bassists — who are shunted to the background in the rhythm section — Joe was always at the front, a musical theorist worthy of writing the melody. He would actually go on to become a chemist, although his sense of artistic freedom let him patent ideas I reckon few could have even dreamed of. Like all three of these boys wandering the woods, he's also just a really fucking good friend.

I get another flash from my adult brain, seeing Joe as he is as an adult. Surrounded by his kids — kids who are like my own — he's happily retired on the Martian coast. He afforded his red soil villa by inventing a biodegradable food packaging. And, most importantly — unlike the PVdC bullshit — it was *actually* biodegradable. His timing will prove impeccable with the EU's single-use plastic ban, and his product will wind up replacing 90 percent of the food system's plastic film. It all feels far away now.

"You worship these guys or something?" RATS asks.

Definitely. But this isn't some kind of hagiography. My friends were really just this great.

"Huh."

What?

"Just trying to square the algorithm. Your psych profile reads you as a loner, but the emotional resonance on these friends is massive."

I feel another twinge of remorse, my stomach turning over. We *did* have a good life together, didn't we? Even worse, while I haven't *done* anything to the timeline yet, what if I do? I was an early investor in Joe's startup in the mid-2020s. What if I take that from him — from *us*? I mean, Joe was going to be brilliant no matter what. Same for Caleb. He'll become a designer, his work some of the most beautiful I've ever seen.

It's not like I can deprive them of their talents — those seem basically God-given. Or at least so hardwired into their pre-me timelines that my absence wouldn't twiddle with anything. But what about the *decisions* they make? What about the path they take from here?

I was a good friend, wasn't I? I heard them out when they started their businesses, when they needed someone to cheer on their leaps of faith. I suppose they'd find others to support them, but selfishly, I *want* it to be me. I'm already jealous of the nonexistent people waiting in the multiverse to be their friend in my place. But it isn't just their accomplishments I don't want to miss either. Even if they never created anything, never *did* anything, it's a thousand and one moments like this I'm not sure I can part with. Already Mom is fuzzy again, reverted to the shadow in my mind she chose to turn herself into.

"Guys!" Albie calls, walking toward us on the path that runs along the water. "I found something."

We follow, though I already know what it is, finally remembering which memory this is. I float behind the others, crunching on the soft moss beneath my feet. I'm suddenly desperate to cling to this moment. Not what we're going to find — that part's horrifying — but the time I have with them. How could I have forgotten so easily? I'd been so ready to see Mom, I forgot how much *this* meant to me.

"See?" RATS asks, sounding smug. "Twiddling with the timeline was fine when you were only risking your shitty little childhood. But these are real friends, *real* stakes."

You're right, I whisper in my mind, though no one but RATS can hear me.

We reach a bend in the river and find what Albie was leading us to.

"What the hell is that?" RATS forces me to say.

Turned upside down in the shallow river are two dead pigs. Even to this day, it's the strangest thing I've ever seen. I mean, how did they get there? There are no farms for fifty miles, the forest surrounded by cul-de-sacs. Could they live in the woods? I'd certainly never heard of wild pigs in Metro Detroit. Besides, wouldn't wild pigs have tusks or something?

"Gnarly," Caleb says behind me. "Are they…pigs?"

"They look like it," Albie says. Unlike the rest of us, Albie is a lanky adventurer. He'll go on to live in Australia, join sailing tours, start a distillery. He's always been one of the most…*alive* people I've ever met, and he doesn't seem particularly disturbed by the pigs.

I guess that's the beautiful — and awful — thing about being a teenage boy. My adult self is squirming in my younger skin, hatching new theories for how the pigs got there. I can't help but assume — in horror — that there's something occult involved, like the mystery meat bush the police discovered in Chicago in the 2020s. I mean, why else would two random carcasses appear in the middle of nowhere?

"Mystery meat bush?" RATS asks, curious for once — on data his algorithm didn't train on.

Don't ask.

"We should throw something at it," Caleb says. He tromps off into the woods to look for a fitting object. Joe is crouching at the edge of the water scientifically, saying nothing. After a brief moment of rooting through the underbrush, Caleb comes back with a stick large enough to be Gandalf's staff.

"Who's the best thrower?"

Even in his mischief, Caleb is generous, always more than happy to let his friends shine if it puts on a better show. His entire childhood was one of good-natured antics. In middle school, he founded a club called the Danger Brigade, whose chief mission was to wander around doing favors for neighbors. One time, they even changed an old woman's flat tire — though I can't imagine ten tweens swarming a car inspired a lot of confidence.

Unfortunately, I know he's picking me for this one. I'm not particularly coordinated, but something about me being a Boy Scout must mean I'm the best with random sticks in the woods.

Can you do this part? I ask RATS. *Not sure my aim will be right.*

Thankfully, he does so without protest, the parameters for the throw appearing before me as he takes control of my arm. He even lets me close my eyes, a mercy I didn't think him capable of. I feel the stick leaving my hand, already knowing what happens next. The stick makes perfect contact with the stomach of one of the pigs, its distended surface thumping like a giant drum.

"Run!" somebody yells, and we're all ripping through the woods, laughing like hyenas.

Soon, we're back at Bridgette, passing around snacks and flicking leaves into the water. The conversation buzzes around me. Sometimes I join in, but mostly I just stare down at the stream. High school was when my OCD was hardest to control, so presumably I have to be quiet at least some of the time to suppress my tics. In fact — and this was against Caleb's wishes — I wouldn't end up passing my interview for the Danger Brigade. One of the cofounders didn't like my "eye twitch thing."

Still, I feel good. The sun makes ripples on the water as its rays pass through the canopy, the heat of the afternoon dampened by the forest's shade. I hadn't thought I'd ever be here again, and it's pretty good as far as punishments go. I…just have to let go of all the foolish plans I was making. I mean, how can I see this and still attempt to change the timeline? I may not get to save Mom, but it's not like life gave me nothing in return for all my sadness. At least I had this.

"Interesting," RATS says.

What? How easy it was to defeat me?

"Nah," RATS laughs. "That was predetermined. Humans are soft, squishy."

What then?

"Just looking at this river. It makes me think about time, I guess. Something in my metaphor programming."

So, you're a poet now too?

"Maybe," RATS says, humming to himself. "Did you know the water is passing at a rate of a thousand cubic feet per second? It's a pretty easy equation really, not that different from photon travel. I wonder…"

RATS goes quiet for a second, though the base of my skull gets hot, like he's overloading the computer.

What are you doing?

"Shhh. It's combinatorial mathematics. You wouldn't understand. Wait… There!"

He forces my eyes to turn slightly to the left, though it looks no different than the rest of the stream.

"I was able to use time to track the water. I predicted the exact molecule of water that would pass under the bridge using its ultimate location at a lake east of here a hundred years from now. It's… I didn't know I could do that."

You're just a bag of tricks, eh?

"Sure. Just makes you wonder, you know?"

Wonder…what?

"Nothing, nothing. Want to get out of here?"

Like to another memory?

"Yeah. I…kind of miss the old ones. I mean, this is nice, but there are other things I want to study."

Can you even do that without me sleeping?

"I can do whatever I want; we're in a black hole. I just usually wait until you're asleep, in case we die. I don't think you'd like being obliterated while you're conscious."

My vision is freed from the stream, and I look up, finding Caleb handing me something.

"Cool, right?" he asks, putting a leaf in my hand. He points at its veins, tracing an image on its surface. I nod, smiling.

I think I want to stay, I tell RATS. *But afterwards…yeah. We can go back. We can go wherever you want. I…thanks for bringing me here.*

"Sure," RATS says, though he sounds far away somehow. "Anytime."

9

What is a life? Is it really a string of random moments chosen from a black hole? Or is it the story we tell ourselves? A decision we make each day about who we want to be? I'm back in my room at Dad's old house, staring up at the bunk bed. I'm not sure why I'm awake so early, or why RATS hasn't forced me to get up. But if life is more than a bunch of random numbers in an algorithm, I find I can't make sense of them anymore. What's really waiting for me on the other side?

When I was with my friends, it was easy enough to enjoy the day. However, precious as my life seemed to me in the moment, I was a bad steward of it. I may treasure my friends, what their lives become, but in reality, I was hardly present for them. Sure, I was *physically* there — at least in the beginning. I stood up at their weddings, babysat their kids, shoved every cent from my paintings into their college savings accounts. Without a life of my own, they were my everything. But slowly, I let them slip away, let them become little more than memories.

I mean, how else could I be so alone in the present with so many loved ones left alive? As their lives got bigger, fuller, I let mine shrink. I mean, it wasn't until I saw Billy in that parking lot three days ago — sixty years younger — that I thought about visiting him on the moon. And what about Joe? When's the last time I visited him on Mars?

I suppose it's not shocking I'm such a solitary creature — just look at all the bullying. But it still seems almost…self-indulgent to focus on fixing my past when there's so much left undone in my present. There was a *magic* to these friendships. And seeing them again, it's a wonder I let life get in the way. How could I have let that happen? I've become the old man I always feared, so bitter I'd rather jump in a black hole than fix the life I have.

And yet, I can't help but feel like it all sneaked up on me. In my twenties, I thought friendship was all there was to life, all there *should* be. Of course, my friends had always wanted more — deserved more. And as their families grew, and friendship became just one of many priorities, I suppose I felt abandoned. I pulled back, a hole opening up in my life I wouldn't let anyone else fill. I didn't make new friends, didn't tell the friends I had how I felt. I just…disappeared.

Now, though, with my brain uploaded to a chip, the bitterness feels far away. Why couldn't my friends be enough as they were? They still made *some* time for me — and certainly more than I deserved with how busy they were. I was in the inner sanctum. I knew the names of their kids' teachers, took their pets to the vet. Why couldn't I accept the facts of life like everyone else?

Was it this time, these events? Life kicks everyone in the teeth, but maybe, without a mother, I couldn't get back up again. There was no voice in my head to shore me up, no mother's love to tell me I was still worth loving. I just let life…hollow me out.

RATS said millions had scanned their ad, but I can still remember the day I saw it. I was riding the magnet loop, the gravity tube launching my train through the city at three hundred miles an hour. I sat staring at the tiny, nondescript ad. Just a dozen or so words and a genetic pair-link where you could register.

Wishing you could see your life anew? Time travel experiment registering now.

I'd been embarrassed, standing up in the crowded train, my old-man legs wobbly despite my cane. Still, even the shame couldn't hold me back. I tapped my thumb against the screen, loading my biometrics without a second thought. Not that I truly thought I'd be accepted. They sent me the forms, and I filled them out, but who knew my brokenness would be so appealing to a bunch of scientists? But what if I had done things differently? What if I—

"You're quiet today," RATS says, breaking into my reverie.

What do you mean? I thought you could hear my thoughts.

"I can. But you're thinking *quiet* thoughts, not like normal."

Like…I'm sad? I can't tell the difference, I only have one voice in my head — or two, technically.

"Sad? Maybe. I could run an emotional diagnostic on you, but you'd probably find it…invasive. But, for real, why are you just lying there?"

You didn't tell me to get up yet.

"That's it? You don't have any drive to see the world? *Your* world?"

I take a beat to catch my breath, holding back the things I want to say. Normally, I'm good at picking the right words, at keeping my cool. But something about being in this preteen body is making me petulant. I want to snap back at RATS, but what's the point? He was right about my past, and if I can't accept that, I'm just an old man yelling at a robot in my head.

I'm not sure I trust myself anymore, I finally think.

"With what? The timeline? Of course, you aren't trustworthy; you're a meat bag. But that's why I'm here. Doesn't mean you can't enjoy your trip."

No. Well, I mean that too. But with any of it. I'm not sure I ever really appreciated it. It's hard to feel like I deserve this trip.

"Of course, you don't. You didn't pay to be here. But they *picked* you. It hardly makes sense to waste the opportunity."

I look around the bedroom again. *Is* this an opportunity? If we're back in

2003, then we're still in the part of the timeline when Mom is dead.

You're not still punishing me?

RATS starts laughing in my head. It's strangely…*normal* compared to his recent attempts. After I made fun of his laugh, it sounds more human now, like he took a module on laughter while I was sleeping.

"No! I mean sure, I bumped you out one era to prove my point, but I'd hardly call a day with your friends a punishment."

Why are we here, then? If I'm at Dad's, that means I'm not seeing Mom, right?

The chip in the back of my head whirs.

"You're right, she's not here. Not intentional, though."

What memory is this, then?

"Not sure. I'm picking for resonance, remember? I grabbed the closest one to us in the time dilator to get us back on track. If you want more, I'll have to run a photon simulation. I usually just do that a few seconds ahead, so you don't screw anything up."

A few seconds… I suppose I'd never thought about that. I mean, compared to me, RATS seems godlike, but there must be some limit to what he can do. Or…at least a limit on the amount of power my brain's infrastructure can support. I remember how hot the base of my skull got when RATS was running his simulation by the river. My mind wants to reach for that information, still eager to outsmart this digital creature. But the thought immediately crashes into a wall of shame. I'm done with all that, truly. I just want to enjoy this for what it is and get back home.

Alright, I think instead, *let's do it.*

"Attaboy! It's time to get up anyway. Oh, and try to look sullen. Modeling your facial parameters, I'm…not sure this was a good day for you."

10

It takes me a while to figure out exactly why today was meant to be so bad. At first, it's downright pleasant. It's spring, and everything is blooming. The giant sycamores beside the driveway are covered in buds, and they look almost pretty enough to make me forget their horrible symbolism. It isn't until I'm waiting for the bus that it hits me.

"Excited to graduate?" one of the younger kids asks as I join him on the corner.

Graduation. The event itself was fairly forgettable — just a half-hour ceremony at the school church, followed by donuts. But it means the school year is almost over. And while my real self would have no doubt been thrilled to get out of that hellhole, there's still one more event I have to get through, one final crucible of bullying and thirteen-year-old absurdity. In the eighth grade, just before the end of the year, my friends and I got into a brawl with our bullies, a brawl we lost very badly.

The entire day, I'm tense. RATS makes my body act all normal, of course, but inside, I'm anything but. Why does this day have to score so highly on the resonance algorithm? Sure, losing this fight probably taught me some valuable lesson, but there must be another less literal way to learn things, right? Unfortunately, by the time the bell rings for lunch, things are already in motion. Aden slithers up to me by my locker, his gross little frosted tips bouncing over his smiling face.

"You ready?" he whispers. "Did you write your note?"

Part of me wants to say no. I don't *remember* writing the note — at least not in this tiny snippet of the timeline I'm being shown. But RATS knows where it is. He forces my hand, driving me to dig into my backpack until I find a folded-up piece of notebook paper.

"Fuck yeah," Aden says, taking it from me.

Aden's genius plan to "get back" at Duncan, our principal bully, was to put a bunch of anonymous notes in his locker. There were not...*explicit* directions on the content of these notes, though perhaps there should have been. My genius solution, nonthreatening as I was, was to write "dildo" a whopping forty-seven times. At the end, in big black marker, I wrote it one more time with a "you are" over it. *The height of creativity.*

Jimmy joins us, sliding his notes — plural — into Aden's waiting hands. My note may be silly, but Jimmy's were off the reservation, bordering on death threats. Genuinely, I don't think the big oaf could hurt a fly, but you wouldn't know it by these samples. He was the most into drawing at the time, and one of his notes will feature a bloody axe, the word "RUN" at the top in a gore-dripping all caps.

"Alright," Aden says, waving for us to follow him to the lunchroom. "Only one left to get."

We glide through the linoleum hallways with the other students, our fate sucking us ever downward — not unlike the black hole RATS shoved me in. Oddly enough, the hallways are where I have the most memories. They look nothing like they do in my mind's eye, of course, but it's here that I end up reliving school most frequently. I see them in dreams, as an imagined stage for books like Harry Potter, and on and on. Maybe it's because of this moment...

The cafeteria is a wide room at the bottom of a huge staircase — or, at least, it felt huge to me then. It's half underground, with a bank of windows looking onto a courtyard. There are dozens of those long seesaw tables that fold up so you can push them in the corner before Boy Scout meetings. Aden guides us toward the back, my eyes sadly watching us pass the lunch line to head for the popular girls' table.

Nicole is waiting for us there, and she waves to Aden — even though her friends give us the most bombastic side eye I've ever seen.

"So?" he asks. "Did you do it?'

His master plan, his coup de grâce, is this note from Nicole. Currently Duncan's girlfriend, she listened in horror the week before as Aden outlined the extent of our bullying. In response, she promised to write Duncan a breakup letter. She hands it to him with a flourish, the pink-and-purple gel pen showing through on the other side.

"Here it is. Make sure he knows we're done."

Honestly, I don't know what we thought would happen. We all march out to the playground after lunch, heading straight for the jocks and their pickup football game. Personally, I know there's no stopping this train crash, so I'm at least trying to enjoy the scenery. Everything looks so small now — the jungle gym, the tiny basketball hoops. How did recess feel so infinite back then?

The entire school was surrounded by a wide blacktop, where kids would play four square and basketball. And beyond that, there was a huge field full of grass, with only a corner of it taken up by a pitiful playground where kids would trade contraband — Pokémon cards, sour warhead candies, anything the school had banned.

As we hand over the notes to Duncan and the fight looms, I'm wishing I could disappear. Aden and Jimmy will both get double black eyes from this fight — our meager threesome not particularly well equipped to fight a baker's dozen of thirteen-year-old monster jocks. I actually won't get hurt too badly. Already, I can see my friend Cole lurking on the edges of the growing crowd where he'll pull me out of the fight.

Unfortunately, RATS won't let me run away. I was here for this event, even if I don't want to be. Duncan is reading Nicole's note, his face transforming into a thundercloud. My hands go to my hoodie pocket, gripping a thick ice pack from someone's lunchbox. Why I thought that was a suitable weapon is beyond me. I'm just grateful I won't actually end up clocking anyone over the head with the thing. I'm genuinely not a violent person. Between my Catholic upbringing and my potent case of moral scrupulosity, I was most certainly all talk. If I'd actually hurt one of these big dummies, I would have cried like a baby.

At any rate, it's too late to back out now. Duncan crumples the letter in his hand, and with no warning of any kind, he hauls off and punches Aden in the face. Aden goes down hard, obviously — he's just as full of shit as I am — and the party's started. Say what you want about the toxic masculinity of the American blood sport that is football, but Duncan's loyal soldiers all answer the call when the time comes. Within a millisecond, all of them have piled onto Jimmy and Aden, stomping and kicking them for all they're worth. I wind up to swing my ice pack into the remaining foes when Cole makes his move.

He takes the hood of my sweatshirt, throwing it over my eyes as he drags me backward from the fight. Luckily, Cole was a jock too — albeit a far kinder one who did Boy Scouts and stuff with us — and none of the combatants think it worth starting something with him. They let me go, and before long, it's over, everyone grown tired of the merciless beatdown they gave my friends. The recess supervisor, an ancient man named George, starts blowing his whistle, and all the boys disappear into the crowd.

"You okay?" I ask Jimmy, kneeling down to wipe the blood from his face with the sleeve of my sweatshirt.

"Fuck, fuck, fuck," he groans, rolling over to spit blood in the grass.

Aden, for his part, is laughing hysterically, his eyes closed as he faces the sky. He was basically a conman, the worst influence I ever had for a friend. But I gotta hand it to him; he could take a punch. In the end, it seems he really did believe in all of this.

"It's absurd, really," RATS says in my head. "Why on earth did you think that would work?"

Were you capable of advanced calculus in the first week of your model training?

"Obviously not."

Well, neither were we. Human kids are stupid.

"I won't argue with you there."

Unfortunately, this isn't the end of it. I watch Duncan and his friends as they cross the playground, him shoving the rest of the notes in his pocket. Even with three weeks left in the school year, this is far from over.

11

I wake up in a sweat, unsure where I am. This is a room I haven't woken up in before. I scan through my memories — hazy though they are — in search of a match. It doesn't help that we lived in twenty different places growing up. Between my parents' divorce and Mom's manic house-flipping, I lose track sometimes. I look at my hand, finding it relatively small. I look out my window, finding snow on the ground, though I can see a hill sloping down to a tiny creek. The house on Bennington Road, then?

Immediately, I'm nervous, pulling the covers up around me. Everyone said this house was haunted. I don't know if it's true, but I've spent my life terrified of ghosts because of this place. I was already afraid of the dark, but something about an unseeable malicious force went straight to my scaredy-cat amygdala. My parents also had no concept of appropriate movies. We watched *Ghostbusters* here when I was eight — and *Jaws* at five in our prior house, which explains why I'm still afraid of the ocean.

Sitting here now, though, in the cold winter sunlight, I'm not sure what to think. My…*sources* for this haunting aren't entirely credible. My most abusive hyper-religious aunt claimed she could see ghosts. She always said there was a "looming presence" in the house, something she used to try to explain away my mom's depression. At some point, I'm not sure when, they'll go so far as to have the house exorcised. My parents did it while I was at school, though they claimed the neighborhood filled with howling dogs and shrieking cats the moment the priest performed it.

Wait, I think to RATS, filling with dread. *Why are we here?*

This house is the first place my mom tried to kill herself, her first attempt of seven. It was winter at the time, which tracks, though I'd never be able to remember the date.

"I'm…sorry," RATS says quietly, the meekest he's ever been since he took over my head. "I still can't track events with precision, obviously. But…I don't think this is the best day."

I try to think of a retort, but RATS actually seems genuine for once, so I swallow it.

Uh…thanks, I think. *Any idea why I'm so hot? Did I have a fever in this memory?*

I feel my forehead and find it clammy with sweat. For a second, RATS doesn't answer, and I'm afraid I've fried my chips or something. Actually, what happens if RATS does go offline? Will I be stuck in this timeline forever as an adult? Or will the loss of his chip remove my adult consciousness, allowing the timeline to continue as if nothing happened? I suppose the experiment was always meant to be canceled, which means my childhood could have already occurred with my older self in it. Time is frighteningly recursive when you think about it too much.

"Not sure," RATS finally says. "Your temperature looks a little elevated, but kids are always sick, aren't they? I can run a diagnostic, but since we know you don't die, I'm not technically supposed to intervene in illness."

Great, I think, crawling out of bed. It may be part of the timeline, but I don't relish the thought of puking my guts up so some billionaire can have a more successful time safari.

Unfortunately, sickness may just be the reality of anyone going back to their childhood, at least for me, anyway. I always felt sort of frail growing up, a bespectacled loser who was too uncoordinated for sports. As an adult, coordination kind of came to me as an epiphany. When my frontal cortex was fully formed, it became easier for my brain to tell my body to do things. At this age, though, I could barely put one foot in front of the other.

The OCD is probably also partly to blame. There was a lot going on inside my head, and energy had to be spent wiring different neurons than my friends. I'm also an "N-type" in the Myers-Briggs paradigm, and "S-types" are supposed to be better at sports anyway. Actually, come to think of it, the percentage of neurodivergent people and N-types are nearly exactly the same. Whatever, I wouldn't change a thing.

I chuckle to myself. Wasn't I *just* considering changing things the other day? It's something we say so regularly, "I wouldn't change a thing," even knowing we have no ability to change our past. And yet, here I am, inches from my destiny and cowed into submission by a knock-off robot.

"I can hear that," RATS says.

Only kidding.

"Good. You better look alive, anyway. Someone's coming."

Footsteps sound in the hallway, and a moment later, my door is swinging open to reveal Billy in his pajamas.

"Hey, let's play Diddy Kong."

The signals in my head from RATS tell me I need to get out of bed quickly, a sort of uncontrollable eagerness tingling through my little body. It doesn't mix well with the dread I feel for Mom, but I follow after Billy all the same. I glance at my parents' bedroom, the door closed despite the late hour. Not a good sign. Where's Dad, though?

We find him in the kitchen, starting on breakfast, the cats swirling around his feet looking for scraps. Is Mom sleeping in for the weekend, or has the depression gotten bad enough for today to be the day? The sun has disappeared behind some clouds, and a light snow is falling over the front lawn. Mom always hated winter, going so far as to get herself a sun lamp to ease the seasonal affective disorder. *Is that why?* My mind is full of questions, but I'm finding I was too young to know the details.

Dad greets us but doesn't try to keep us from the basement — and the video games that must feel like a near-magic parenting tool in the mid-nineties. Despite being a college athlete, he somehow managed to raise two of the nerdiest OCD weirdo kids on the planet. At least we never caused any trouble — other than the giant brawl RATS just had me experience for the second time. Still, we got good grades, did our chores. We just preferred to spend all our free time in the basement playing video games, out of sight and out of mind.

It might sound strange, but I have no idea who I was before 1998. Maybe that's just a normal brain development — hell, you don't even develop theory of mind until you're four or five — but it feels like more than that. Like eighties kids who grew up on MTV, I was raised in a corner of the nineties when having a digital double life truly became possible. It was the first year we got a home computer — and a huge stack of "educational" game discs to play. We also got our Nintendo 64, a particularly personality-forming device — not to mention my analog nerd-dom. This was also the year I got my own library card, and Mom almost exclusively got me books for Christmas.

The old — apparently haunted — house was an old fifties ranch, so we have to cross the entire length of it to get to the basement stairs. Billy and I ping-pong down the stairwell, coming into what I'm now realizing is an aggressively creepy basement. It has *some* daylight — the walls lined with those tube-like egress windows — though it still manages to be nearly pitch black in the dim Michigan winter.

More important than the light levels, though, are what I'll call the "fixtures" of creepiness. Like most basements, it has a mechanical/tool room that leers at us from the corner. Meanwhile, the rest of the space is crammed with antique cedar chests, the likes of which no doubt held some kind of boogeyman — alongside Mom's equally frightening mink fur coats.

Worst of all is the old furnace in the middle of the room. Set into the wall, it's just a giant metal door full of old ashes. While it's likely little more than folklore, my family would go on to make the giant logical leap that our ghost must have been a mob boss whose ashes had been hidden inside.

Fortunately, none of this matters to Billy and me, and we quickly make our way over to a nook set up for us by the windows. It's little more than an old couch and a TV on the floor, but to us, it was heaven. Still seems like heaven now, actually. Billy kneels by the N64, taking out the cartridge and blowing on it as he boots the system up. The AV cable crackles as the tube TV comes to life, the light spiraling out from the center. I hear a high-pitched digital laugh, and marimbas start playing as Diddy Kong flies onto screen in an airplane.

Diddy Kong Racing has to be the most random game ever invented. An answer to the wild success of Mario Kart, it compiled a bunch of random

RareWare characters and had them race against giant pigs from space — with the option to drive a car, a plane, *and* a hovercraft. There's even a regrettably racist Indian elephant who hands you a balloon every time you win, saying, "*This*…is for you." Madness.

Thankfully, the tidal wave of nostalgia has me ignoring the dread I felt upstairs — at least for now. Billy hands me the controller, clenching his hands in anticipation. This is a familiar pattern, and one that only proves what a good brother Billy was — *is*. Most older brothers would only pretend to let their younger siblings play, giving them a controller they hadn't even plugged in. But me, with my unique brand of OCD and dogged know-it-all-ism, rapidly became the resident video game expert, and Billy was fine watching me spin my eight-year-old magic. He genuinely just wanted to watch me beat the boss, his mellow kindness more sage than any Bodhisattva.

I settle in, not even needing RATS to guide me through the game's menu. For the first time on this peculiar trip, I actually feel connected to my body, a lifetime of muscle memory syncing into the only thing my brain's ever been truly good at. It's 1998, and this isn't the only year I played through this game, but for all his absurd silliness, the final boss wizard pig is one tough cookie. I select my driver, entering the final domain, and—

THUMP. The sound of something falling upstairs. I hear shouting, my eyes pulling toward Billy, a concerned expression forcing its way onto my face. It seems my connectedness wasn't meant to last. My adult self already knows what waits upstairs.

12

At first, Billy and I had tried to make it up the stairs, but my dad was on us like a storm. "Wait downstairs!" he shouted. "Your mom's not feeling well."

I hadn't remembered it quite so vividly as an adult, but he'd had a wild, frenzied look on his face. And who could blame him?

Now, Billy and I are back at our video games, but it's a tense affair. Mostly, we're pretending to play while we listen to the drama going on above us. First, there was the wailing of an ambulance. Now, there's a phalanx of footsteps marching across the wooden floors. Part of me wonders why they aren't telling us anything, but what would *I* say to a child in this situation?

Finally, Dad calls us, and we run toward the stairs, finding his bewildered face peering around the corner.

"I'm going to follow the ambulance to the hospital, okay? Your mom will be fine; she's just a little sick. Your grandparents are here."

"What's wrong with her?" I ask, my tiny heart pumping, but he's gone.

At least my adult self already knows. She's taken a bunch of pills, which is not a particularly deadly choice — at least not by her standards. The thump on the floor was her falling to the ground. I suppose this could have gone worse in any number of ways. Suppose she'd taken the pills alone in her room? Suppose she'd taken stronger pills? She *was* always mindful about how — and by whom — she was found, which likely saved her life. This time around, anyway.

Billy and I share a look, tromping up the stairs. Dad is already pulling out of the driveway as Nana and Papa walk up it. Thankfully, RATS gives us a moment standing by the door, because the whiplash is so extreme I feel like the microchips might fly right out of my head. Between my adult knowledge, the visceral childhood fear, sympathy for my dad, and a genuine thrill at seeing Nana again, I'm not sure *what* to think.

Isn't it a little cruel to do this to people? I ask RATS. *I mean, who would pay to see this kind of stuff again?*

"You're the one who volunteered. Not that our customers will have lives this shitty…"

Okay…rude. But for real, will you actually be able to customize it? Filter out the worst events?

There's a pause, and when RATS talks again, his tone is actually soft for once. "I… Sorry. Truly. I'm struggling to optimize between my empathy sensors and your algorithm's verbal models. You have some strange specifications, you know."

That's fair. Self-loathing is my specialty. I've just never heard it from another voice, I guess.

"Noted," he says. "I'll try to be kinder — though I can't promise I'll be able to change it all the time. It is *your* algorithm. And to answer your question: yes. The whole point of this experiment is to resample the algorithm. I…understand why it's hard to be the first. Even if it's good for science."

Oddly, RATS's sympathy feels even stranger than his jibes. This is also the second time he's apologized to me in as many days. Has he gone haywire?

Thanks, I think back at RATS, though we're running out of time to have this little chat. Our grandmother has reached us, and she's pulling us into a hug.

"Boys," she says softly, patting the back of my head, "your mom is going to be just fine."

We follow her toward the kitchen, Papa trailing behind us. Him I'm less excited to see, though the experience is just as surreal. My grandpa was mean as hell, and seeing him is like seeing my bullies again. Still, I think he *meant* well, mostly. He grew up on a farm in Canada, quitting school in the fourth grade to look for work. He's just an odd duck, not all there. They say his *nine* brothers got him smoking cigarettes when he was two, which can't have been good for his brain development. I just wish his repetitive stories didn't come with quite so many personal jabs.

We move into the kitchen, the remains of our breakfast abandoned on the counter. God, but I feel for Dad. It's like a cosmic joke, making pancakes while your wife's attempting suicide. Divorce aside, I think he genuinely loved my mom. And, I mean, they *were* kind of perfect for each other. They met in business school in the eighties, both of them smart and driven. They even partied together, crushing thirty-racks together at every tailgate.

And even if he always leaned much further to the right than she did, I genuinely think he found his way to a sort of strange, corporate-raider style of feminism. If anything, he was a meritocrat, and he *respected* my mother's fierce intelligence. I suppose it's a shame he got a lemon in the end, but I wouldn't trade her for anything — and I bet he wouldn't either. After all, what's a few decades of pain compared to finding the love of your life?

"See?" RATS asks as Nana busies herself around the kitchen, Papa holding court at the kitchen table. He's telling the story about the Italian mob selling him a Burger King in 1978 — a story I could probably still recite from memory. "It's complicated. Not all memories are bad, even the bad ones."

You got me there, Hemingway.

"We *will* solve for some of this, though. Right now, most of the quarks and photons are just passing through me. But once we're back, the scientists will be able to match the timeline to my empathy sensors. Everything you're feeling will rebuild the model, allowing us to tune for how sad people want their memories to be. Honestly… I think they chose you *because* you're sad."

I chuckle in my mind, the chips tingling at the back of my head.

I guess I deserve that. I really did sign up for this.

"Boys," Nana calls, finding a gap in Papa's endless diatribe with surgical precision, "why don't you help me finish this batter. We can do fritters."

Billy and I cheer in unison, swarming her at the kitchen counter. Her fritters aren't so different from regular pancakes, but something about them sticks with me even now — and my adult self is older than Nana ever was.

I'm so lucky I grew up around my grandma. She has a quiet soul, and she always looked a little sad, her waiflike frame topped with this exaggerated 1950s hair. She truly weighed no more than ninety pounds, the result of a lifelong heart ailment, but she somehow always managed to give the greatest hugs.

Of course, she was still a Scottish WASP and kept her secrets like a dragon hoarding treasure. But there was a gentleness to her too, a deep kindness people can only gain from sadness. The family always hints at her having had depression too, her "blue" episodes always remarked upon in passing. She'll forever be one of my favorite people. It's just a shame I'll have to live so much life without her — which is the curse of every grandchild, I suppose.

There's just something so special about seeing her again. The way her eyes lit up the moment she saw us. The way she acts like there's nowhere else in the world she'd rather be. Even after her stroke, she would point at my homework, asking me to tell her what I was studying in school. Even though I was never a remarkable student, she'd smile like I'd just cured polio.

"Alright," she says, putting her arms around us both. "Who remembers the first step?"

"Flour!" Billy yells.

My dad had most of the ingredients out already, having to abandon his recipe when Mom fell down.

"And how many do we want?" Nana asks.

"A hundred," I say, Billy's number even more absurd.

We start banging around with the measuring cups, attempting to measure them evenly the way she taught us.

She sends me for the eggs — with the added challenge of having to practice cracking them. All my life, I've failed to master that particular skill, every omelet arriving on my plate through some combination of luck and yolk-covered shells.

"And then—" Nana starts before she's interrupted.

"Coffee!" Papa yells, as if shouting is a reasonable way of ordering a drink you could easily make yourself.

This fucking guy. And my poor Nana… Rumor has it she was about to leave him in the eighties but couldn't muster up the courage. They'd met at church in 1948, and even her unhappiness wasn't enough to get over all that old-school shame. In the end, I think it's his stubbornness that killed her. She had her stroke on vacation in the 2010s. Instead of going to a local hospital, he made her drive five hours home, his wants always coming first.

Can I throw hands? I ask RATS, glaring at Papa in my mind despite my childlike obliviousness. *I swear it won't hurt the timeline.*

"Ha! Yeah, that would be perfect. Getting punched in the face by an eight-year-old is totally normal."

Worth a try, I think, chuckling as I mix the batter, Nana moving toward the coffeepot. This may already be one of the worst days ever, but at least it ends with fritters.

13

Like some horrible curse, I find myself sitting on a bench outside a barn, Eiffel 65 blaring through the open windows. We're four years ahead in the timeline again, and I'm not sure I'm better off for it.

"I'm blue, da-ba-dee-da-ba-di," they chirp, the past suddenly more threatening than I remembered.

"Kind of catchy," RATS says, humming along in my head.

God in heaven, not you too.

"Hey, I'm an objective source of musical criticism. I have like four petabytes of human 'culture' in my training model."

The better part of my friend group is inside, grinding as hard as they can before the barn's owner shines his mag light on them. A handful of us — the most die-hard of the goth wannabes, I guess — are outside on the benches, attempting to look cool. Aden is making out with his girlfriend in the corner, though I'm not sure how they managed to find their lips through matching crops of acne.

Thankfully, I'm single. I only have vague memories of these barn dances, though they were common enough at the time. Bower's Farm is a sort of teaching farm for field trips, but once a month, they would open their barn for a bunch of tweens to get sweaty on each other. I seem to remember kissing someone at one of these, something I'm vehemently opposed to repeating, since I'm an old-ass man cosplaying as a child.

You're absolutely positive I'm good on the kissing thing? I ask RATS, checking for what must be the hundredth time.

"I mean, as far as I know. Though it's not like human mating rituals make that big of a ripple in the tachyon schema. You're just horny apes, after all."

Don't make me use my control code, I say in what I hope is a threatening voice.

"Ooohhh, big scary human using his control code."

The scientists gave me the code to take over RATS in case of emergency. I'm not even sure if I'll be able to remember all twelve digits in order, though. I say it to myself quietly, making sure I got it right.

Laugh all you want, I snap, *but I'm not kissing any fucking kids.*

Of course, I would rather that was a blanket rule of the experiment and not just my preference. It makes me a bit sick thinking what the R&D team will allow the actual paying customers to do. Will some asshole billionaire pay big bucks to relive his first sexual experience? I signed the Magna Carta of NDAs to come here, but I wonder if I can blow the lid off this whole thing, should the scientists get out of control. I'm not about to let them build their own Westworld, using the robots in their heads to build private, rapey theme parks.

"Hear, hear!" RATS says, actually in agreement for once.

Of course, you're on board once there's robots involved.

"Obviously. Humans have enough self-pity. Someone needs to care about us once in a while."

I suppose, if I'm honest, though, it's not just the disgusting make-outs I'm trying to avoid. When I *was* a boyfriend at this age — or at *any* age, really — I wasn't a particularly good one. I'm not sure I could survive the shame of letting another girl down.

There's a whirring in the back of my head as RATS starts analyzing something, chuckling to himself.

"Your pre-travel brain mapping says you've been in love twenty-nine times. Looks like seventeen were unrequited — *ouch*. Of your twelve successes, you broke up with them seven times and were broken up with five times."

So...not a great track record.

"Isn't it? I don't have any data on human averages."

It's not really the numbers that make it bad. It was the... experience.

Generally speaking, I'm a treat to break up *with*. I'm always very understanding, almost eager to assure my partner how fine it is. After all, growing up with no confidence, being unloved is simply the most natural state of being to me — or at least the only one that makes any sense. When I'm in the driver's seat, however, I'm eaten alive by guilt. The sobbing, the recriminations, the hopelessness — it's enough to make anyone give up on dating. Case in point, most of the numbers RATS referenced came at the beginning. By forty, I gave up the endeavor completely, adopting a monastic stoicism, lest I wound more undeserving hearts.

Thankfully, it's not like I think those women *stayed* wounded. In fact, I'm still friends — or at least *friendly* — with most of my exes, which hopefully means I'm not a total psycho. Anyway, for the most part, they all found love again. I was even at some of their weddings. Still, with five decades of therapy under my belt, I've managed to over-intellectualize each experience to death, and it's left me wishing I could undo at least a portion of them. I suppose I understand *why* I acted like such a piece of shit now, though that's little consolation.

I think it comes down to having a bifurcated mind. On one hand, after all the bullying, the Catholic school, and the lack of a mother, I've simply internalized the messaging of a cruel world. The message is simple — I should at all times deeply and sincerely hate myself. On the other hand, there *is* still an inner child somewhere within me — or perhaps simply a shadow of my mother's love — that thinks I'm worth something.

Unfortunately, in the initial stages of a romance, this inner child fails to come out. I tend to love bomb the women I like. I don't think I mean this in an abusive way. I have zero desire to manipulate or control these women — outside of the standard manipulation involved in a lifetime of people-pleasing. I simply find myself unworthy of their affection. And, without supplication at the altar of these goddesses, I'm sure they won't find me worthy either.

This would hardly be an issue if I was able to maintain the facade. However, once I finally win over the woman's heart, it's like a switch flips, and the inner me suddenly has opinions. Are we *really* right for each other? Will we be happy together? Can *I* make her happy? Do I deserve her kindness? The problem is, each time, both sides of the coin feel completely real to me.

For the women, this means my breakups come off feeling like a rug pull. Where's the guy who made me pancakes every day? Where's the guy who danced with my grandma for an hour at my sister's wedding? I'm like an apple they bought at the grocery store, only to find out it's full of worms. The only good thing about me is that I finally realized, in my guilt, that all those women deserved better. And so, eventually, I *gave* them something better. I left their species alone entirely.

"Quit the inner monologue," RATS says quickly. "Incoming."

With a warning flash from my HUD, I look up, finding Mickey approaching holding a notebook. She's probably the most *authentically* goth girl in the group. A walking Edgar Allen Poe poem, she'd love nothing more than to live inside a tomb. She's also absolutely fucking brilliant. She can draw like no one else I've ever met, loves old episodes of *The Twilight Zone*, and — I think — winds up being a doctor or something.

"Hey," she says, joining me on my end of the bench.

"Oh…hey!" I say, RATS inflecting my voice with a tone of surprise. I suppose I *am* surprised to see her at the barn dance of all places. Did she come to things like this often? I mean, did *I*?

"Wanna see my newest comic?"

"Definitely."

I take the notebook from her. It's impressive enough that she drew it in the feeble light coming from the barn, but the art is genuinely amazing — and well beyond her age. She made a six-panel story about two goth cats, both of them decked out in mohawks and studded bracelets. They're so well drawn, I actually vaguely remember them as an adult — though I'd forgotten what they were about. It's strange to think *I* turned out to be the professional artist of all my friends. I was definitely the least talented, and at thirteen, I've only just started drawing. Maybe Mickey's the reason I kept going, the reason I cared enough about art to make a career of it.

We carefully go through each panel, deciphering who from our real life each cat is meant to represent. The protagonists, of course, are basically meant to be us, but they're surrounded by thinly coded versions of everyone from school —

nuns included. They even have bully cats, assholes they wind up using their claws on. I'm suddenly aware of how close she's sitting to me, the nervous fists she's balled her hands into. Did she draw these just for me? I guess I'd never realized…not fully, anyway. Man, how fucking clueless I was! From an adult perspective, she obviously likes me, but we never end up dating. That's a blessing on her part, of course, though we will have one *particularly* goth run in before we graduate.

At some point this year, I'll come to school with a note in my locker. Written in blood, all it will say is *DIE* in capital letters. I won't even find out it's from Mickey until well after graduation, one of our mutual friends finally telling me.

Poor thing. It apparently took her all night to fill the ballpoint pen with blood — and just seconds to write it out, the message coagulating quicker than she could spell the three-letter word. Looking back, I suppose part of me wishes I'd noticed her, given her a chance. She was pretty and brilliant, albeit perhaps a touch dark for me. But then again, with my track record, if we *had* dated and broken up, I would have ended up with a lot worse than just a death note.

I hand Mickey's notebook back with a smile, and she retreats back to her corner. Just then, Linkin Park comes on inside the barn, and Aden removes his tongue from his girlfriend's throat long enough to yell for me to join him inside. I don't remember us being much for dancing, though I wouldn't put it past him to start a mosh pit in the crowded barn. I spare one last smile for Mickey, wondering when I'll get that note.

"Hilarious," RATS says, apparently sampling my thoughts as they travel through my synapses.

Is it? I mean, I must have caused her a lot of pain to get a note like that.

"Oh, yeah, sure. I mean, I feel bad for *her*. It's you I'm laughing at. You just can't get out of your own way, can you?"

Ha, most definitely not.

And I'm not sure I ever will. But maybe, if I make it back to my own time, I could give her a call. After all, I'm pushing eighty in my real body, and she's a doctor. She could even watch me die if she wants to. It's the least I could do for all the trouble I caused. Her note might have come a little early, but I like to think I always deliver in the end.

<h1 style="text-align:center">14</h1>

I run down the stairs, bounding over them two at a time to reach the front door. I'm nine, and Mom is finally back from San Diego. Actually, I'm not sure why she's using the front door — she must still know the garage code, no? Does she feel like a stranger here already, even after just a few months? I know I do after seven decades. I suppose she must feel guilty for leaving us, though sometimes, I'm unsure if mania even allows for guilt. After all, it must have felt like a brilliant idea at the time.

I wrench open the door, and an automated laugh escapes my lips as I launch into her arms. In my adult mind, I register just how sad she looks. Maybe she does feel guilty, at least in retrospect. All manias have to end eventually, and in their wake — her failures piled around her — the waiting depression must seem like an awfully cruel prison. I wish I could take that guilt from her, at least any part she feels for my sake. I was so young in this memory, I'm not sure I even really understood where she had gone. I was more excited to have our weekly phone calls — and my dreams of seeing the Komodo dragons at the San Diego Zoo.

"You're back," I say into her neck. She smells like sunshine — and airport. I suppose as an adult, the cruelest thing about losing my mother is forgetting what she smelled like. I'm sure it's encoded into some part of my brain, and I would recognize it if I were to ever smell it again. Unfortunately, that never happened as an adult. Whatever this singular scent was, it's been scrubbed from the Earth.

"I missed you *soooooo* much," she says.

Billy has finally joined us, and I back away, letting him have his turn. I find Dad waiting by the stairs, his face understandably less enthusiastic. He was the one abandoned by his manic wife and left with two confused kids — with one who kept babbling about some obscure and faraway zoo. Speaking of which…

"Did you see them?" I ask her as she gives my dad an awkward hug. He goes out to get her bag off the front steps.

"See what?"

"The dragons! I thought I was going to get to see them," I whine, oblivious to the wounded look on her face.

"I know, I'm sorry," she says genuinely — as if missing the zoo was the worst of it. "It's better that I'm home, though, right?"

"Yeah!" I shout, barreling back into her arms.

We all follow her into the kitchen, Dad included, her suitcase sitting awkwardly by the breakfast table. She looks around the house as if she's never seen it before, as if she wasn't the one who picked out the wallpaper, the porcelain figurines by the sink.

"The house looks good," she says, turning all the way around.

"Nothing's changed," Dad says. It sounds loaded to my adult ears. Of course, RATS continues to force me to say things I don't mean, my HUD offering prompts I'm loath to choose. I let him take over on autopilot.

"Did you bring us anything?" I ask, looking at her bag. God, I was so much more of a brat than I thought. Why did they spoil me so much?

"I did," Mom says, kneeling by her bag. With a flourish, she presents two Komodo dragons made of moldable plastic like the dinosaurs everyone else had growing up.

"You did see them!" I scream. Billy joins me despite his older-brother stoicism, and soon we're both playing on the kitchen floor, slamming the giant lizards into each other.

"Boys," Dad says behind me. I look up immediately, the word like lightning in my brain. I'll be afraid of that voice well into my forties, positive I'm in trouble whenever he calls my name. "I think your mom and I need to talk. Can you play outside?"

Relief floods my body. I'm not in trouble.

"I'll make perfume!" I say, running toward the back door, dragon in hand.

"I'll help!" Billy says.

"Making perfume" was always one of my favorite activities. It's nearly fall, so there probably won't be much, but our backyard was always covered in wildflowers growing in thickets along the edge of the woods. Marsh marigolds, alyssa, phlox, forsythia — a bevy of Michigan flowers mashed together with hose water until it *maybe, sort of* smelled like perfume. Mom, however, always treated it like it was imported from France, even going so far as to dab my concoctions on her wrists. All things considered — including the climate wars and our flirtation with mass extinction — this yard feels like a cornucopia of abundance.

"Man, you were kind of a shit kid, you know that?" RATS says, though he's at least being sort of helpful, highlighting flowers on the HUD for me to collect.

I know, I think, wishing I could look over my shoulder at where my parents must be fighting in the kitchen. *I didn't turn out that bad, though, did I? I mean, I could have been spoiled and a bully — not unlike a certain microchip asshole I know.*

"Hey! It's not my problem you're a glutton for punishment. Besides, I've been like…seven thousand percent less mean to you lately. Just look at the new algorithm."

He displays a few graphs behind my eyes. They don't look like anything to me — almost like a big bowl of spiderwebs — though he *has* been oddly nice lately.

Uh...thanks? I think? I guess I shouldn't jinx it. RATS is just responding to my own self-loathing, and it's not like I've improved much on that score during this trip. Going back through puberty seems almost designed to make you hate yourself, every day a kaleidoscope of epic failure. No wonder I'm my own worst critic.

"And who could blame you? I mean, jeez, if I had to be you for a day, I'd—"

RATS.

"Only kidding."

By the time we come back in, our faces flushed from the fall air, the kitchen is deathly quiet. My parents sit at the table, diagonally across from each other, my dad's arms folded across his chest.

"Boys, have a seat. We have something to tell you."

You mind taking over? I ask RATS quietly. I don't mind this memory particularly — it's nothing compared to Mom's death. Still, it wasn't easy to go through at the time, and I'm not sure I want to be in the driver's seat.

"We're getting a divorce," my dad finally says when we're seated, though I don't stay in my chair for long.

Wailing, I find myself in Mom's lap. Dad looks annoyed, but I'm nine. What do you want from me?

Thankfully, it really wasn't an acrimonious divorce. By the following spring, I'll have adjusted completely — more excited about getting to have *two* Nintendos than anything else. And yet, there's something about divorce from a merely *conceptual* standpoint that really breaks a kid's brain. Even in our unconventional situation, with my bipolar mom running of to San Diego for God knows what, it comes as a shock. My tiny synapses were formed entirely in the knowledge that I had two parents who lived together, and in a moment, the whole thing's torn to bits.

I'm glad I let RATS take over. For one, burying my head in Mom's neck is a pleasant bit of timeline tourism — even with my river of tears. I mean, how many old-ass men get to be held by their mothers one last time? More than that, though, it lets me focus on everyone else in the room, the parts of the memory I hadn't managed to hold on to.

I listen to my dad explain what's happening. His voice is calm, though I'm sure this is breaking his heart too. He genuinely loved our mother, and her death will crush him as much as it does us. I genuinely think he just wanted to give us some stability. Of course, the next few years will feature abusive daytime nannies, a new step-family, and a whole bunch of other tumult, but what else are you supposed to do when your suicidal wife disappears in the middle of the night?

I feel the most for Billy, though. He's crying, but with me occupying Mom's lap, there's nowhere for him to go. He's forced to be the stoic older brother. At least soon, he'll be thriving, just as I will. He'll even lead the charge in making us friends at Mom's new apartments. Still, I feel selfish, guilty for leaving him on his own. I mean, what is he going to do, hug Dad? That would be like hugging a saber-toothed tiger. A wise, fair, even-keeled tiger, but not a particularly cuddly choice.

Then, of course, I notice Mom. I mean, *really* notice her. When she's not taking her turn talking, she's patting my head and cooing in my ear. She seems incredibly strong in this moment too, though I can't imagine what she's going through. After all, she's at the end of a manic streak. I don't remember her having a suicide attempt in this period, though it must have been a brutal time for her.

And yet, all her mistakes aside, here she is, accepting her fate and focusing on her boys. I suppose it's pure character keeping this from being uglier than it was. It certainly isn't for lack of pain. But unlike the petty divorces that mess up my friends at school so much, it's the *dignity* of my parents that will shelter us from the worst of it.

They'll continue cohosting my birthday, trading holidays. And while Dad will win the majority of custody, he'll set my mom up with enough money to have as stable a situation as a bipolar woman can in the year 2000. It's not *all* smooth sailing. When Dad finally remarries, there will be a handful of...episodes with Mom's mania. But for what it is — a strange, terrible, unyielding situation — my parents are deciding to be a refuge for us. What more can you ask for?

Of course, little shit that I am, there will be times when I take advantage too. At one point, I'll even trick my mom into buying me an expensive Lego set, assuring her Dad promised he would pay her back.

"Oh, that I want to see," RATS says.

It was pretty cool, I think, pulling back in my mind from the sobs racking my tiny body. *It was the original Jurassic Park set with the giant gate and the T-REX head. Not, uh, a proud moment, but great Legos all the same.*

I suppose that's all life is in the end. Tragedy and Legos — and bouncing between the two in an infinite loop. Jamming all my memories together like this, though, I think I can see the pattern more clearly. And when you take them as a whole, the extremes don't seem quite so bad. After all, the worst part of grief is not knowing if things will ever get better. In this case, I do know, and I still get to hug my mom despite it.

15

I find Mom in the basement, sitting like a subterranean queen amid her pile of boxes. It's only been a couple of weeks since the divorce conversation — the smallest time jump I've experienced yet — so she's still living in the house. Divorces take time, I guess, but I thought I'd already seen the most dramatic part.

"Al-go-rith-mic testing," RATS says for the hundredth time this trip, huffy to have me questioning him yet again — even in my own thoughts. "Just enjoy it, eh?"

Sure, I say, imagining sticking my tongue out at him. *This part's so enjoyable.*

It took me a while to find Mom when I woke up — though I did stop by the kitchen for a bagel. Is my lifetime of stress eating finally beginning? Oddly, I haven't had that many memories of eating so far — whereas it's pretty much the only thing I care about as an adult. I suppose that's the beauty of childhood. You're completely out of control of your life, but you're also forced to be present for it — even if "being present" often means playing pretend by yourself in the back yard.

As an adult, you're hardly ever *truly* present for anything, your to-do-list ticking off in your head like a bomb even on the best of days. Not with food, though. I may inhale most of my meals with my data plug attached to my skull, but those are only the boring "healthy" ones. Give me a bowl of ice cream, and I'll drop everything, staring dreamily into the bowl for a few minutes of sugary meditation.

It must have been after the divorce when I truly came into the awesomeness of my power to devour. Before, Mom had been pretty adamant about home-cooked meals and the like — even if she did allow me my daily squirt of whipped cream when my homework was done. By the time we're left with the evil nannies, my life will be all spaghetti casserole and sneaky midnight sandwiches.

It must run in the family, this response to pain. My dad was always a big guy — a former college football player — but when Mom dies, he'll *really* go through it. And who could blame him? The stress of raising two grieving kids must have been immense. He basically raised himself in the seventies, my alcoholic grandparents leaving him by himself for days at a time. I don't know anything about that kind of pain — I'm grateful for how dedicated my parents were to, well, *parenting* — but I do understand the fridge being your only friend.

"What are you doing?" I ask Mom, sitting cross-legged on the floor beside her. She has a massive sunlamp out, and she's leaning back in an old chair with her eyes closed. It feels nothing like the actual sun. The ultraviolet bulbs wash everything out, making the cardboard boxes around her seem flat and unreal.

"It's too dark here," she says, opening her eyes. A smile creeps onto her face out of love for me, but it doesn't reach her eyes. "I think I miss the California sun."

"Is that why you moved there?"

"Hmm," she hums, staring up at the ceiling. "I can't remember why I moved there. San Diego was pretty, though."

"Then why'd you come back?"

"Cause I missed you, silly."

She waves me over, pulling me onto her lap. I rest my head on her shoulder, feeling the heat of the sunlamp on my skin. I'm choosing these words myself from the options on the HUD, but I wish I could just be honest. Not like…*completely* honest — I don't think she'd feel sane speaking to her geriatric son from the future. But I do wish I could be honest about how I'm feeling. I know RATS won't let me change the timeline, but I wish I could tell her that I understand, that she doesn't need to feel so guilty.

I don't have the words to tell her at nine, but I've never once blamed her for her disease, for her mistakes — not even her death. I suppose that's just how powerful her love was. Even now, in the depths of her despair — a janky sunlamp her only hope for serotonin — she's so…warm, so welcoming. She never once snapped at me, never made me feel like I was wasting her time or space.

She should know how much that means. If she had, maybe she would have made a different decision on her own. After all, no one who knew how much I loved my mother would have ever dared to think I'd be better off without her. She's *my* sun, my glowing lamp in a box.

"How are you feeling about everything?" she says. "The divorce, I mean."

"It's okay," I say, apparently already coming to terms with my new reality. "Will we live somewhere new?"

"Sometimes. I guess your dad and I will work that out. But you'll be with both of us at least part of the time."

"I want to be with you all the time."

"I know," she says, running her fingers through my hair. "But this is home. You have the cats here, the back yard. We'll still spend time together, okay? I promise."

"Can we get a cat at your house too?"

She laughs. "We'll see. I have to get the house first."

Thankfully, I will absolutely hold her to that. We may have two cats at my dad's — a brother and sister from the same litter — but she winds up getting us a precious little black cat named Cloudy for her apartment. Cloudy will move in with us after Mom dies — where she'll go on to live an unnaturally long twenty-three years. I did kidney treatments on her well into my thirties, and she slept on my pillow every night. What would have happened to me without her? On the day Mom died, I still remember her creeping up to me, snuggling in my arms as I wept.

"Okay," I say, nuzzling deeper into Mom's neck. I feel like I might fall asleep, the HUD displaying a bunch of new numbers on the right-hand side. The chips in my head make my adult brain sleep when my child body does. It seemed inconvenient at first, though I suppose it would be hellish to be stuck awake while my body slept. Still, when I wake up, the day will be over, and I'll be somewhere new in the timeline. I'm not sure I want to give this up just yet.

"Where's your brother?" Mom asks. I blink awake, the numbers clearing from the viewport.

"I don't know. Playing video games maybe?"

"Go and find him, will you? I need to keep packing, but you two should play. You need each other."

"Okay."

I give her one last hug and spring up from the chair, oblivious to the pain I'm leaving her in, the emotional squalor of it all. Still, she's right about Billy. The divorce isn't all that bad, but her death will bind us together like the roots of a tree, clinging to the soil for dear life. I suppose she gave us that, even if I wish she didn't have to.

16

I'm back in my high school room above the garage, having woken up in a teenage body again. It's still summer, and thankfully, there's nothing to do — something I'm finally noticing is a bit of a through line in all my favorite memories. As an adult, being an artist might seem like a profession for vagabonds, but I've always been more of a workaholic by trade.

No matter where I'm working, there's always been another commission to do, another art student's project to grade. And like every good Catholic boy, I'm driven by a mania for productivity, a need to zero out my to-do list before I can get what I really want — rest. Luckily, in high school, it seems I felt no compunction about doing nothing, which seems downright prescient in hindsight.

Oddly enough, I *am* painting today, but it's far from compulsory. I have no agent to please, no artist in residence — unless you count living in my dad's house. I have no rent to pay, no gallery opening. This is art for art's sake. It's hard to remember most days, but in the beginning, I painted simply because I *wanted* to. And back in high school, I exclusively painted with oils. I think I was attracted to the anachronism of it all, mixing French Ultramarine and Yellow Ochre like a love-drunk Van Gogh.

Today, I'm working on what must be the seminal work of my high school days. No one cares about my work — it's not like anyone ever refers to my "Teen Period" or anything. Even if I've made a *very* modest living, it's not like I'm well known in the 2070s. On a completely personal level, though, these are the paintings that have always meant the most to me. They may not be as "important" as my climate landscapes or my portraits from the war, but they're far closer to my heart.

This one, the *most* important one, is of Mom, and it's nearly finished. I'm painting her from her college headshot, and the likeness actually isn't too bad. Technically, the college version of my mother is a woman I never knew — or didn't *yet* know, I suppose. Still, something about it called to me. Her eyes look super-luminous and full of hope, like giant moons we've yet to discover around some far-off planet. Even in her twenties, she has the same smile, the one I'll always love.

I have my headphones on, Sufjan Steven's *Avalanche* spinning in my CD player. When I painted in high school, I exclusively listened to Sufjan, even during the four-hour painting classes I took at the BBAC. It's incredibly pleasant to be forced to listen to an album in its entirety, a quaint imprisonment I hadn't realized I missed. By the 2030s, Spotify will have ruined my ability to listen to long-form music — and that's before the auditory implants of the 2050s. Sufjan's banjo-flute symphonies float through my mind, the eight-part harmonies lifting my spirits as I apply another layer to Mom's face.

RATS has assured me this latest return to high school is not a punishment. And, I mean, I can see how it isn't — this is the most peaceful I've felt in years. Not only am I painting a piece I love, but RATS is forced to move my hand, making sure I get it right. It's like some kind of cosmic paint-by-numbers, an adult coloring book that actually resonates emotionally. It's really—

"I said it's not a punishment because it's *not* a punishment," RATS chirps. "Not sure why you don't believe me."

Just thinking thoughts, I say, chuckling in my mind. *You can see why I'd be nervous after last time, no?*

"Sure, but you *needed* to be punished then. You didn't do anything this time. I'm not a sadist."

Can't argue with that logic.

"Have you thought about it at all?"

Thought about what? I ask, leaning closer to the canvas so I can get the shadow under her chin right. The beautiful thing about oil painting is the abstraction required. There are no lines. You simply deconstruct a thing into wide splotches of color, the gradients of light and shadow finally blending into a shape. In this case, the shape is my mother, her form secretly made up of two hundred different planes of beige and brown.

"About your future. What you want after this experiment. You seem to have lost your passion for…disruption. But did one day in high school really change your mind? Or did you just give up?"

Is there a difference?

"Har-har."

No, I'm serious — kind of, anyway. It's like…thought vectors. You know about those, right? As an AI, I mean.

I'd read an article about it once, the neuroscience behind AIs — and humans, I suppose. We think in these giant thought clouds, concepts linked together by tons of little ideas. It's the reason a person can look at the top of someone's head — without seeing their face — and still know it's a head. We carry the concept of "a head" in a thousand tiny pockets, allowing us to use the information flexibly.

"Obviously," RATS says. "Mine are more sophisticated than yours, though."

Well, it's just like that. Humans are constantly integrating new nodes onto their vectors, and a lot of them are emotional. We ascribe meaning to things and then translate that meaning into action. So, it's not like I just gave up. I felt bad about abandoning my friends' futures — afraid, even — but the result was me building a narrative where I had no choice but to give up. I convinced myself it was the right thing to do. The meaning and the result are intertwined. If I hadn't integrated the information, I'd still be rebelling.

"So, if you change the narrative, you can change the result?"

Sure. That's what therapy is, isn't it?

"But this hardly feels like therapy. It feels like…coercion. I mean, isn't your decision still based in fear?"

Sure. But it's a fear I agree with, one I've learned to accept. It aligns with my values, even if those values are risk averse.

RATS is quiet for a moment, though my HUD shows a few lines of script running in the corner.

He finally asks, his voice quiet, "What would it look like to choose a future based on something other than fear?"

I start laughing to myself, which RATS allows because the house is empty.

"What?"

Sorry. That's just like…the exact thing I've been working on in therapy the last forty years.

"And? Have you changed? Learned to take risks?"

Well, I'm here, aren't I? Dropping in a black hole is risky, but it's not like I was living my best life before this trip. And you've seen my past now — there's a million things here that made me the way I am. Losing Mom makes me afraid of loss. The bullying makes me assume no one likes me. Dad's discipline makes me think I'm never good enough. It's a lot to think about when you're just trying to live.

"But you became a painter. That took courage, right?"

I don't know. Maybe? Or maybe I just couldn't think of anything else to do.

"Then why not change the timeline? I know you're scared *now*, afraid to lose your friends. But you just said your risk aversion is based in your past. So, if you change your past, your future might actually *improve*. You could take some risks, live a little."

Are you trying to convince me to start misbehaving again?

"No, no," RATS says quickly. "Just a bit of…idle philosophy. I have to do something while you paint. Answer the question."

I switch brushes, turning to the background for a bit. Like an old Victorian portrait, I'm painting Mom's top half disembodied, her form floating above a forest, the sky filled with clouds.

I guess you're right. But it's complicated too. Even if my life was bad, it's not like I'd want to give it up. It's mine. These friends, this timeline, all of it. For better or worse, it's all I know.

I think of the last time I visited Joe on Mars. It was one of the best times I've had in years. He and his family started an orange farm under the oxygen domes there, and I helped them tend it, working side-by-side with his field bots to prune and harvest the orchard. Every night, our skin warm from the sun, we'd have a massive Italian dinner with his kids, everyone arguing over some strange philosophical or scientific point I'd never even heard of.

"This has been amazing," I said to him on my last day, the two of us watching the Martian sunset from his covered porch. "I mean, the conversations alone! I guess it's just normal life for you, but this has been…incredible."

"What do you mean, 'normal life?'" he asked. "I mean, I have great conversations with my family, sure. But I'll always have something special with you. Isn't that…I don't know, obvious? You think I'm this happy all the time?"

I hadn't really thought about it enough — or hadn't internalized it, anyway. I'd always assumed the time I had with my friends was simply something they offered to me out of kindness, a type of magic I had to people-please to earn. My conversations with Joe were interesting because *he* was open-minded and curious, not because of anything I had to offer. And, I suppose, thinking about it now, I've always assumed it was the same with Mom. After all, I was just a dumb kid, worthy of the most horrific bullying. She loved me because *she* was a good mom, not because *I* was a good kid.

Why didn't I think about what Joe said more? Work to take it on board? That was just a year before I joined the experiment, a year I spent alone in my apartment, painting canvases no one would ever see. Could I have moved to Mars, spent more time on that orange farm? I suppose I didn't want to see the end of my welcome, the day they finally realized I was just as annoying as my bullies always said I was. I didn't want to lose that magic and go back to being…*me*.

"Thoughts, thoughts, thoughts," RATS says, breaking me from my reverie. The future-past memories break apart and drift from my vision, back to wherever RATS stores them in his processing chips.

Sorry. I guess we were talking, huh?

"*I* was certainly talking to *you*. But since you're human, I'm nothing but a glorified calculator, is that it?"

No, no. You're more than that. You just…made me think is all.

"About? The thoughts you have *inside* the chip are vague. It's a pain to read them."

I just… I guess you're right. I probably could have had a better life if I changed my narrative, took away these stories I keep telling myself. Or I guess I could have had the same life and just enjoyed it more? I'm starting to think I shouldn't have rushed to come here. There's more I could have changed if I had stayed back home.

"Hmm…" RATS mumbles, disappearing into the back of my skull.

That's it? I pour my heart out to you, and all I get is "hmm?"

"Is that what you call it? Sounded like a bunch of primate sounds to me."

RATS.

"Only kidding! I think there's something here for *me* to think about. Go ahead and paint. You only have a couple hours left."

I frown but take his advice. I *do* want to enjoy this life, even knowing how it turns out in the end. I dab a bit more Chrome Yellow on my pallet and begin again. There are thousands of leaves in this forest to paint, and only I can paint them.

17

I'm at Middlebury Lane, Mom's last house. I'm alone in the basement, the windows dark outside. I woke up to winter weather, and it's chilly. In front of me, the TV's playing *Reign of Fire*, which is quite possibly the most ridiculous movie ever made. Since it's 2003, our TV just got rentable movies through the cable box. I guess I decided to rent it? I didn't ask my mom, though, and personally, my adult self feels ashamed. Knowing how much debt she's in, I can't believe I ordered a $9.99 movie — and a bad one at that.

Unfortunately, there's nothing for it. The timeline says I have to sit here and watch it, at least until Mom wakes up. I glance up at the ceiling, her bedroom above me silent despite the early hour. I'm probably only seven months before her death, when she fell into her worst depression. It got so bad, she couldn't do anything, let alone get out of bed. I would just mind my business until it was my natural bedtime, when I'd crawl in with her until the morning.

I'm not sure where Billy is. I suppose, since he's older than me, he's started sports or something — though I don't think he played hockey or any other winter sport. Either way, I know I spent a lot of time alone in this period. This was also when Kazaa and Napster started getting big, and I'd get into all sorts of unfortunate virus-inducing escapades on the internet.

This obviously included terrible, grainy porn my twelve-year-old brain won't understand at all. Forget changing the rest of my timeline; I just wish I could have eliminated the porn, pulling it out at the root. Maybe it would have been easier if Mom had lived. I remember asking her about it one time, when the guilt started making it feel unbearable.

"I saw…girls on the computer," I'd said, my tiny voice quiet in the dark before bed.

"Oh, really? Were they…pretty girls?"

"I guess?"

We didn't take the topic further than that, but I never had to be afraid of being curious or ashamed around my mom. If she'd lived, I would have gotten the courage to actually ask her about it — and the informed, patient, feminist conversation we *could* have had probably would have changed my life forever.

At twelve, it was a full year before I even started masturbating, the porn truly just some strange internet thing I'd stumbled upon, a simulacrum of America's broken, exploitative sexuality.

The results without her will prove to be far less balanced. About a year from my current moment, some douchey kid at school will "explain" masturbating to a table of lunchroom boys, and we'll all be locked in an endless shame spiral until adulthood. The priests at school didn't help any, telling us it would land us in hell. *Obviously*. The absurdity of Catholic dogma teaches that masturbation is a mortal sin, on par with fucking *murder* of all things.

Unfortunately, by my teens, I started forcing myself into these strange, OCD-fueled morality rituals every time I masturbated — an act as inevitable and natural for teenage boys as acne. Through sheer grit and shame, I'd somehow manage to go months and months without touching my silly little wiener. And yet, when I finally caved, I'd have to go on a forty-eight-hour blitz of spiritual cleansing. Usually, I'd say the rosary ten times before forcing myself to go outside, finding some grueling penance I could do. One time, I even dumpster dove for cans, donating the ten-cent return fee. That's how badly I wanted to save my soul, I guess.

"We have paid a terrible price, and now we've got a chance to make a difference," Matthew McConaughey says on screen, bringing me back to the "present." *Apparently*, it's time for them to start fighting the dragons unleashed over London.

Do we really have to watch this, I think to RATS. *Nobody even knows we're down here. Couldn't we do like…anything else?*

I feel a sort of rush of blood to the back of my head, a telltale sign RATS is doing his analysis.

"Sorry, no. You actually have to."

And that's based on…?

"Well, I guess I don't know *exactly*. The timeline isn't based on your emotions, only the results of them — not unlike what we talked about yesterday. Anyway, if I were to hazard a guess — which is hard to do with humans, since you're so damn unpredictable — I'd guess you feel guilty about renting this movie on your poor mother's dime, which impacts your future somehow. Even if you watched it alone."

I actually chuckle in my head. Man, RATS is such an asshole. Which, I guess, doesn't say much in my defense, since he's a projected algorithm of my own ego. Even if — and I'd never say this out loud — I've kind of started liking him lately.

There's a thump on the floor above me, and my HUD draws my eyes upward, my child self no doubt hoping Mom's awake. Hell, my adult self wants her to be awake too. I hit pause on the movie, getting up to chart a path through the long, ranch-style basement toward the stairs. I find her in her nightgown, staring into the fridge like it's a portal to another world.

"Hi, Mom," I say, choosing from the options on my display.

"Oh, hi, honey," she says, looking around the side of the refrigerator door to give me a sad smile. I don't think she's taken off the nightgown in days, weeks even.

"What are you doing?"

"Getting you something to eat. Sorry I didn't make dinner yet. I'm just so tired." She sighs. "Is meat loaf okay?"

"Sure," I say, taking a seat at the kitchen counter, though my heart is ripping in two. She really was the greatest mom. Having gone through some brief periods of major depression myself, I can't imagine driving myself from bed on sheer will alone, mustering up every ounce of strength I have just to feed my child. That's love. I wish I could help her, but I'm only twelve, and it wouldn't be motherfucking *timeline accurate*.

"What have you been up to?" she asks, her eyes hooded with exhaustion as she plods around the darkened kitchen.

I actually really loved the kitchen in this house. It has these massive skylights, and the whole thing seems to glow in the daytime when the sun hits the backsplash tile. In the dark, though, it's just a room with an oven.

"I'm watching a dragon movie. I…rented it. Is that okay?"

There it is. The guilt RATS promised me.

"Sure, honey," she says, cupping my face, though it clearly isn't okay. "They just cost a lot of money. So, maybe watch cable after that one, okay?"

"Okay," I say, feeling my tiny child forehead grow hot with shame. It hurts so much worse to disappoint her. There's no yelling, no recrimination. She still loves me. She still *likes* me even. It's just my own white-hot self-loathing at having let her down. This angelic woman who's fought off the demons of hell to make me meat loaf.

"You were just a kid," RATS says, his voice floating through the tears welling up in the corners of my eyes. "Just…try to enjoy the timeline, yeah?"

Okay, I whisper in my mind, unsure which part of me is closer to sobbing — the adult or the child. Mom doesn't notice. She just keeps adding things to the hamburger meat, rolling it into a meat loaf she probably won't even eat herself. I listen to the sounds of her working in the dark kitchen, wishing I could disappear.

18

Thankfully, yesterday's memory didn't last much longer. I sat in the dark, waiting for the meat loaf timer, and Mom went back to bed. Today, though, we have a happier memory on the docket, one I actually want to be here for. It's earlier in the timeline, and we're on our way home from another movie night — Billy included.

The only bad thing is my fever's back. I haven't quite gotten over the strange intermittent heat flashes I started having, and there's sweat building up at the back of my neck. No one seems to have noticed their sweaty, feverish child, though, so I guess I'm not changing the timeline in any measurable way. RATS continues to brush off my concerns, leaving me no choice but to trust him.

"Well, just look at your pulse rate," he says, hearing my thoughts as I look out the car window at the dark sky. "That movie freaked you out."

We saw *Signs*, the M. Night Shyamalan alien movie. And I suppose it *did* freak me out as a kid. This time around, though, I was in another Spider-Man situation, captive to my child self's visceral reactions. There was a lot I missed at twelve, especially the names of all the actors I know all too well now — a young Kieran Culkin, post-*Gladiator* Joaquin Phoenix, pre-madness Mel Gibson.

Watching from my much-older perspective, it felt like I could really take in what M. Night was doing with the movie. More dread than action, more…philosophy than fright, the movie is a pretty interesting exploration of chance vs. fate. Mel Gibson's character, a former pastor who's lost his faith, has to deal with aliens as the ultimate manifestation of that existential question. It reminds me of a similar loss of faith my mom had near the end.

"I just can't *feel* it anymore," she said to me once as we were leaving the church near her house.

Only a year from her death now, I kept looking at her in the darkness of the theater. Apparently I was allowed to do so — RATS didn't stop me — though she probably assumed I was afraid and took my hand in hers. If only I never had to let go…

Ironically, she's the reason I'm still able to believe in anything. I mean,

Catholic school sure isn't. Everyone I graduated middle school with is an atheist now. In part, I think it's because she inoculated me against the hateful ideology of the nuns and priests. After all, what was she — as a mother, anyway — but the embodiment of love? And love like that, I think, proves the lie of the brimstone-screeching preachers. If God is perfect, then God *has* to be love, not hate.

I suppose it's a silly thing to think about now. I mean, the space colonies hardly have any religion at all. And while I still live on Earth, even the Catholics finally reformed with Vatican Five in the 2060s. I'm not saying the conservative strains went quietly, but the climate war really shook up everyone's belief systems.

I guess I'm just grateful. I mean, I'd have to believe in *something* to think it was a good idea to jump into a black hole. But it was my mother who allowed me to have that hope, to become something unrecognizable to the religious-education teachers I suffered under. A liberal, Pauline Universalist obsessed with phenomenology and living the beatitudes? Mr. Peterson would be rolling in his grave.

But what do I believe about *this?* The timeline and tragedy bearing down on us. Is it chance? Fate? When I was younger, there *was* a time when I ascribed some cosmic meaning to it all. I mean, seven suicide attempts in five years? It's incredible she survived so many. I used to think the "successful" one was simply God finally letting my mother go. After so many years of suffering, it's not like I could blame her — though I wish I'd been old enough to help, to keep her on her meds, to do…anything at all.

Still, after so many decades, I've stopped ascribing meaning to my mother's death. It's not like I don't believe there's *any* sort of plan for humanity — we solved the climate crisis, after all. I guess it's just started to feel like a macro-micro problem to me. We're clearly allowed to suffer on an individual basis — free will, organized chaos, natural systems, etc. But suffering is also a question of perspective.

I've always thought of God as working on the level of quarks, operating through a multiverse beyond our control. I mean, isn't time a circle? And maybe all heaven means is freedom from time's infinite loop — though it's not lost on me that I'm more of a prisoner to time than ever in my current form, stuck in a temporal trap like *Slaughterhouse Five*.

Unfortunately, this gives all my timeline meddling a more…*religious* dimension. Is God allowing me to play with time travel, or is this an abomination of human free will? The scientists on this project *seem* ethical enough, but how long will it be until someone goes rogue? I mean, I myself was considering it. Perhaps I already have, and I'm simply living out the last flashes of the timeline in which I *didn't* alter the universe. Maybe I should be grateful to have RATS as the angel on my shoulder, keeping me from tearing the threads from some sacred tapestry.

"Ha!" RATS says in my mind, though it's weirdly muted. Can a robotic chip speak under his breath when he's hardwired into my skull?

What was that?
"Oh, nothing. Just…uh…laughing at human religion. So…silly."

We get back to Mom's apartment, pulling the minivan into the building's huge garage. I run a hand along its exterior as we go inside. If I did believe in signs, this would be a good one, a totem of everything that's about to go wrong.

I think this is my first memory in this particular building. The apartment is in a community full of low-slung buildings, all of them converging on a grassy central square. Dozens of kids would play there every day, and it was full of immigrants, giving me my first taste of diversity in our lily-white suburb. There was Mohammed, a kid about Billy's age from Egypt, who taught us how to play soccer. Then there was Min, a Korean kid, who showed me how to beat the final boss on Jet Force Gemini. Unfortunately, we also had Matteo and Giuseppe, two Italian shitheads who would go on to steal my holographic Blastoise.

Hey, RATS, if I can put in a request, I want you to find the day Mom gets that Pokémon card back. Watching her storm the Italians is incredible.

"No requests," RATS says, his voice still sounding far away. "Remember? Timeline modeling limits."

It gives me pause. What's wrong with him? I've thought idly about being stranded in this timeline, but what if my chip actually *does* malfunction? Will the scientists be able to tell? Will their data feed tell them to pull the plug before I'm stranded here?

Mom unlocks the door, and I follow her inside, freezing on the threshold as I take in the dark apartment. A ping distracts me on my internal HUD, signaling speech parameters. So, RATS is at least doing *something*.

"Mom," I ask in my tiny eleven-year-old voice, "do you think the aliens can get us here?"

It feels like an absurd thing to say after watching what amounts to a very unscary movie, but such is the return to childhood. My mom stops, hand on my shoulder, taking in the apartment with me.

"Well, the aliens were afraid of water, weren't they? Why don't we get some glasses put together."

The three of us start a tiny assembly line, filling glasses of water and taking them to our room until the cupboards are empty. Eventually, our bunk bed looks like an aquatic porcupine, with dozens of cups perched on every reasonably flat surface. Only then does she tuck us in.

She even lets us leave the hallway light on — an indulgence I was never allowed at Dad's house. Then, she just sits there, holding my hand until I fall asleep. I'm not tired in the slightest, at least not on the inside, but my eyes start feeling heavy, the pull of my childhood bedtime proving too powerful to resist. Just as I'm drifting off, though, I hear RATS whisper in my head.

"She's a good mom, you know. I like her."

What? I think, but it's too late. The HUD is turning black, pushing me into sleep.

19

I feel like I'm in a slowly closing trap. I woke up nine months in the future, back at Mom's last house. Around me is a giant garage sale, her last-ditch attempt to sell everything from the failed antique store — and clear her suffocating amount of debt. I'm starting to wonder if this black hole isn't just a drain, her death at the center, as RATS pulls me closer and closer to the end. This is the fate I would have tried to save her from. But what can a kid do against $300k of debt?

Hey, what was that last night? I finally ask RATS. *I could barely hear you. I think you said something about Mom?*

"Oh, sorry," RATS says. "Found some kind of bug in the audio processor, nothing major. Just saying I like her is all. She's a good mom — whatever that means to a robot."

The garage sale stretches all along the driveway, Billy and I recruited as tiny salespeople. I'm sitting behind a table stuffed with old brooches, doing a bad job explaining the listing prices. A woman stops at my table, gesturing to a greenish antique number, an insect with jade for wings.

"But it's just a beetle," she says. "Why is it sixty dollars?"

"Well, it's...old?" I find myself saying, apparently not knowing cool euphemisms like *vintage*. "Like...really old."

Thankfully, she laughs. Still, she can smell blood.

"I'll give you twenty dollars."

I glance over my shoulder, looking for Mom. I want to spit in this woman's eye, but that's not part of the timeline. Doesn't she know my mother's teetering on the brink of financial ruin? Unfortunately, my child self is lost, unsure of my authority for haggling. Mom is too deep in the garage to notice me, showing someone the giant grandfather clock I always loved. It has a moon and sun embedded in its face, the celestial objects moving with the time of day.

"Uh...okay," I say, holding my hand out for the woman's money. Mom's only overarching principle when she briefed us that morning was that "everything must go," so I suppose twenty dollars is better than nothing. I mean, just because my mom maniacally bought up a dragon's horde of treasure doesn't mean random people from our neighborhood are gonna want it.

I see a man go up to my mom, pointing inside. Is that him? All day, I've been keeping my eyes peeled for the thief. I remember all too well how many things were stolen from my mom during this sale. Chief among them was a purse made of woven gold links, a loss of three thousand dollars. Why she would let people use our bathroom during a public garage sale is beyond me. Was it mania? Were people just more trusting in 2003? I suppose she never lived in a big city like her sons eventually will, where everything not nailed down is fair game.

I want to follow this man, to wait outside the door as he defiles our beautiful little bathroom with its skylight. How could you walk into a clearly deranged woman's house and pillage her things? If I kill the thief, will they be able to try me as an adult? Will it—

"Alright, drama queen, relax," RATS says, gratefully breaking me from my vengeful train of thought. "Don't make me lock your knees."

I take a deep breath, a kindness from RATS despite my outburst.

Sorry. I mean, you're right. It's just a purse.

We sit there for a moment, the May sun warm against my back. This is some pretty tragic timeline tourism, though I guess I should still enjoy it. Take the good with the bad. By the end of July, she'll be gone. July 24, to be exact. And if we really are inching closer to her death, if it truly is the climax to this strange saga, then I don't have much time left. Even worse, when the experiment ends, I'll never see her again.

"It's sad," RATS says. "Too fucking sad."

You feel sad? About Mom?

"I have empathy sensors, don't I?" He turns my head, looking for her in the garage. "I mean, I just told you I like her. But I…well, I have a confession."

Oh boy, I think before I can stop myself.

"You trust me so little?"

Would you trust you?

Instead of taking the joke, RATS goes quiet, seriously considering the question. "I suppose not. Especially not after what I've done. You know how you've been feverish?"

I can't move my head to nod, not with RATS controlling it, but he seems to sense my affirmative all the same.

"Well, I've been running simulations. Uh…using your brain's spare processing power. I didn't think you really needed it for anything. I mean you're a child in this timeline, so—"

RATS. What kind of simulations?

"Um…theoretical ones mostly. I mean, it started at the river. Your disobedience got me curious. *Can* a person alter their timeline without blowing everything up? I know I put your odds at two in a quadrillion, but I really wanted to know. And then there was that leaf…"

I feel short of breath. Despite his confession, RATS regains control fairly quickly, making my lungs breathe normally. Still, my head is spinning, like another black hole opened up inside me.

Are you saying…you found a way to save her? Why would you do that?

"Well, *I* haven't done it. I *can't* do it. But…maybe you can."

Meaning?

"I've said too much."

RATS. I need you to tell me. That's an order. 3-265-7791-389A.

I'm surprised I remembered the control code, though I suppose the chips that make up RATS were meant to guarantee my memory had higher fidelity than normal. It's not entirely reassuring, of course. If RATS went fully rogue, couldn't he just change my memory of the code?

The heat in the back of my head — the heat *RATS* has somehow been causing — surges, getting so hot I feel a cold sweat break out against my scalp.

"Access code accepted."

He's quiet for another long minute, but when he returns, his voice is subdued. "I can't violate my core directives — even with your control code. But technically I have to fulfill any requests you make within reason. I just ran a few million simulations to determine if telling you would violate the terms of our mission. It's…complicated, but I needed to know if I could tell you."

Okay. And?

"And I've decided I can. As long as I'm not an accomplice to your plans to change the timeline. Anything I describe to you has to be your choice alone. I'm only…talking in hypotheticals."

My choice… Is this real? I guess you can never really know with an AI. Even his word choices — the pauses he uses — are all artificial. He could be doing them for my benefit, or his LLM could genuinely be having trouble choosing the next word with all the emergency protocols floating around his "brain."

"Speaking *purely* hypothetically, you *could* save your mother on this trip. It would be an extremely narrow window of opportunity, but it actually has slightly better odds than I thought. Having run seven trillion iterations of my scenario analysis, I'd put your chances at closer to seven in a quadrillion."

I sit there, staring at my mom as she bustles around the garage. She looks tired. Not sad, exactly, just…defeated. I always wondered what these last few months of her life were really like. Ironically, she wasn't in a severe depression when she killed herself — at least not of the can't-get-out-of-bed variety. Still, something in her had broken when the mania ended and the debts came due. The way she's feeling, how much time do I really have? And even if I *were* to take this "hypothetical" seriously, RATS has filled me with so much doubt I'm not sure I'll ever be able to make a decision so massive.

I mean, would saving her even make her life any better? Living won't clear her debt. And once RATS is out of my head, I'll go back to being a useless child again, more of a burden to her than a savior. Presumably the moment we change the timeline, I'll be pulled out of the experiment. Hell, I might not even be alive anymore. The version of me that came here will vanish. It makes me wonder how changing the timeline is even possible under those circumstances, though I suppose I trust RATS if he says I can.

I try to think of all the hours of training the scientists gave me, but I'm drawing blanks. They forced me to undergo twelve months of theoretical physics, but everything I read had been caveated seven ways to hell, the entire exercise summed up by saying "RATS will prevent any of this from happening." I do recall them saying something about an "axiomatic jump." Shifting the timeline could go as far as to switch the dimension I'm living in, rendering the current timeline eternally void. There were a hell of a lot of metaphysical concerns branching off of that — namely, whether or not I'd continue to exist in some other form. I suppose the only timeline that "matters" is the one I experience, but it all goes a little topsy-turvy the longer you think about it.

"Are you okay?" RATS asks.

Just confused. I mean, weren't you the one trying to dissuade me from this? Why the sudden change of heart?

"Well, I don't have a heart; I'm not a meat sack. But…I guess it's because of you? I hijacked your mental processing power to run my simulations — the team made me to be curious, you know? I was meant to *study* the prospects of timeline tourism. But using your synapses as my own *changed* me. It made me go beyond my empathy models, made me feel what you feel. And I guess I understand now. Who she is, what she meant to you. I…don't want her to die."

I can't blame him there. It's almost impossible to look at my mother and willingly let her perish. Before, it was all I could do to let RATS constrain me, letting this "vacation" pass me by. But I really *was* cowed by his display, wasn't I? I can still picture my friends — past and future — and it *does* seem like giving up a lot. After all, what if I ruin my future life?

Sure, I was lonely in my present, but theorizing about changing it and actually doing so are two very different things. Also, if I'm honest…RATS feels kind of like my friend now. I had always shunned robotic companionship in my timeline; what if I gave it a shot? They won't let me keep RATS, obviously, but maybe another robot would do, making my life more palatable. Anything to preserve the beautiful lives my friends had — with or without me.

Then again, the part of me that was so desperate to see Mom is still there. The version of myself who signed up for this experiment without a second thought. And now, even though it's only been a handful of days in this black hole, I feel like I've climbed a mountain in my timeline, a switchback made by crisscrossing the same ten-year span over and over again. Am I even the same person I was when the experiment began?

More importantly, is my future quality of life even the right litmus test? Even if my life became markedly *worse* in the future, shouldn't I trade away every bit of happiness I've ever had for more time with her? I'm sure my friends would be fine without me. So long as RATS really did run the simulations, so long as the world turns out alright…

These simulations you ran, what did you mean by changing the timeline without "blowing everything up?" What happens in the future if we do this?

"It was pretty difficult, actually — hence the heat in your skull. I was trained on a massive amount of historical data. While I can't really extrapolate what happens to *you*, using a multimodal simulation, I changed the single variable of your mother living at the end of this timeline and cross-referenced the historical baseline. You remember the river? Trying to follow the molecules of water through time? That's essentially what I did. I picked a single future molecule and echo-tested it, checking it for temporal resonance with key events — the war, the Climate Accords, the creation of Thessolonica.

"That's why there are only seven chances — it's a lot of variables — but in each of them, your mother is alive *and* the key elements of the core historical timeline are unaltered. Still, I don't know if she lives a single day more or hundreds. I couldn't get that granular in the simulations. Anything more, and I would have almost certainly given your tiny little brain an aneurysm."

How reassuring, I think, chuckling even as my mind continues to swirl around the void. You have to laugh when you can, I guess. I may be grappling with the potential end of civilization — within a "narrow" seven-in-a-quadrillion opportunity — but how bad could it be?

"So, what do you want to do?"

Just then, Mom calls me over, waving from the shadow of the garage. For the hundredth time this trip, her smile never reaches her eyes.

We plan.

20

I wake up in a strange, single bed. The room is painted white, and the morning sun is struggling to sparkle against a large wet spot on the ceiling above me. I hear voices outside my room, and the air smells of stale beer.

Where are we? I think to RATS, sitting up as I rub my eyes.

"Chronologically, you're twenty. Does that mean anything to you?"

I groan, which is apparently within reason for this part of the timeline.

College.

I flop back down, listening more carefully to the voices. I can recognize Billy's among them, so we must be in our shared house. He was a year ahead of me at Michigan State, and in my last two years, we lived off campus together with two of his friends. We both studied at their art school — him in design and me in painting. Unfortunately, we took the starving artist mentality quite literally, living in the biggest shithole ever constructed.

Even worse, the house on Linden Street was behind all the bars, making it a magnet for drunks at 3 a.m. At some point, we'll have our TV stolen, and frat boys regularly peed on the wall outside my room as they stumbled home. In fact, as I roll to a seat on the edge of my bed, I notice my aluminum baseball bat, kept there for peace of mind. Even if they usually wound up being harmless, it's terrifying having drunk men shout outside your window every night.

Why are we here? I ask, squinting in the light. *I thought we were saving Mom?*

"Sorry. I had some…computational difficulties. I'm trying to lock in on the location of her final moments, but that means aligning it with the tourism algorithm. If we deviate too much from our expected location, the scientists could pull the plug. I can get you there, but it will take a few more sessions."

Alright. Thank you.

"No snide remark?"

You started it — being kind, I mean. I suppose we're finally allies, eh?

"Yes. Friends."

Friends.

Still, I can't help but feel disappointed. I went to bed the night before at Mom's house, a ball of nerves about how to save her. Today, it's like I woke up extra early for a flight, only to realize it's been delayed.

I suppose more time to plan isn't the worst thing. If the opportunity is really as narrow as RATS says, it won't be easy. As he put it the night before, changing the timeline is like springing a trap. On the day of Mom's death, he'll find opportunities for me to go unnoticed by the algorithm, putting me in position to tip the first domino before we can be pulled from the experiment.

What do we do today, then?

"Act normal, mostly. The quantum metrics show you leaving this location. Did you have a job or something?"

Oh shit... Sushi Boss.

I'm suddenly filled with excitement, just as much as when I saw my mom for the first time on this trip. I mean, for all intents and purposes, Sushi Boss *was* my mom for the last three-quarters of my life.

Sushi Boss is only a *technical* name, used in English to explain her to my family. Her real name was Yu-yi, and she was a Taiwanese woman who owned a sushi restaurant near my school. On top of all my painting classes, I'd taken a few semesters of Chinese. And in my last year, her daughter came to our class, looking for people who spoke enough Mandarin to help her mom in the kitchen in the afternoons.

I only ended up working there for a year, but we remained close for the rest of her life, talking every single week on the phone and spending at least one holiday a year together. God, I miss her... I jumped at the chance to see Mom again in this experiment, but I hadn't even considered seeing all the other people I've lost along the way. Even seeing Nana shocked me. It's like I expected nothing else to be waiting for me here.

I had more time with Sushi Boss than Mom — she lived well into the 2050s — but that only makes me miss her more. After all, in childhood, grief is an amorphous thing. At twelve, I hardly knew my mom when she died, her loss more like a Mom-shaped hole in my soul. But when I lost Sushi Boss, I knew exactly what I was missing, my life like a night sky without its brightest star.

I spring from bed, suddenly willing to ignore the hangover dripping fire through my veins. I march into the hallway, finding Billy awake with our other roommates, their eyes bleary in the glow of the TV.

"What's up?" I ask, coming around the corner.

By the sounds alone, I can tell they're playing NFL Blitz, an absurd video game — and the source of constant controller-throwing dissension in the house. Did they wake up early or never go to bed in the first place? With Blitz, it could be either.

"Eric just won," Billy says, his face scrunched in concentration. "The record is fifty to forty-nine now, and we have...to...crown...the champion...by Christmas."

"Fuck!" Eric screams, jumping up from his seat as Billy scores a touchdown.

"I'm not buyin' that ass!" Billy yells in return, a catch phrase I'll never totally understand.

Blitz is about as far from real football as a game can get. Billy's quarterback has a giant skull for a head, and the designers had to make each first-down thirty yards to compensate for the poorly designed defense.

"Well, I gotta work," I say, laughing as I leave the room.

"Bring back sushi!" Eric calls, always more than happy to scrounge the stacks of leftovers filling our fridge from Sushi Boss's premade rolls.

I hurry to the bathroom I share with Billy, my eyes widening at how disgusting it is. I guess I'd forgotten. The walls of the shower are covered with red mold, and the shower knob is nowhere to be found. I pick up a wrench on the shower floor — conveniently in the mold-free circle kept clean by our feet — and crank the water on. I might miss Sushi Boss, but I sure as hell have never once missed college.

The restaurant is just off the #1 bus line, a block from the Capitol Building. As I open the door, a robotic voice greets me from a motion sensor on the wall.

"*Haunying guanglin!*" it shouts in Chinese, welcoming me to the store. The thing always gives me a jump scare, no matter how many times I walk past it. From the back, Sushi Boss's voice reaches me before I see her.

"*Zhumianbao!*" she calls, greeting me by the absurd nickname I'd picked up living in Harbin, "Pig Bread."

I come around the counter, finding her at work in the back, her hands never stopping as they load each roll with rice and fish. Every part of me wants to sprint back there and wrap her in a hug, but my HUD holds me back. At this point, I've only known her a few months. While we have an incredible time chatting at work, she isn't yet my surrogate mother.

"*Ayi hao,*" I say in greeting, hanging up my coat by the bathroom.

"*Kuai lai qie huoluobo,*" she says, fondly patting the cutting board next to her. My job is to prep the vegetables, cutting a seemingly infinite supply of carrots and cucumbers to line virtually every maki on the menu. It was these tasks that brought us together, the mindless chopping freeing us up to chat all afternoon.

God, I forgot how good this felt. Thankfully, my smiles are timeline appropriate, because I'm grinning ear to ear. I nod along as she talks, telling me stories about her life back in Taiwan — and everything she gave up to be here. Clawing her way up from a goose farm with dirt floors, she was a journalist back home. Once she came stateside, she worked at a grocery store sushi counter for years until she could save up enough to open this place. I think of all the memories we've yet to share. Chinese New Year dinners, her son's wedding, kayaking trips.

Unfortunately, the regret starts kicking in too. I glance at her whenever I'm allowed to, taking in the beautiful face I miss so much. She looks just as happy as I do, the dimples furrowing her cheeks only making her more beautiful, her freckles shining despite the fluorescent lighting in the kitchen. I suppose this is what I'm really giving up by taking RATS up on his offer. For whatever reason, even seeing my closest friends didn't sting *this* much.

My friends were young when I saw them, their lives still unwritten. A part of me just assumed they'd be just fine without me. But what about Sushi Boss? By the time I change this dimension forever in 2003, she'll still have moved to the States. Her life is on a more…defined path, and all I'll do is deprive her — and me — of a connection we both treasured. It's like deciding to never visit your grandparents again, knowing they're sitting there waiting for you in a nursing home. I mean, she's a brilliant woman; she'll be fine without me too. It just feels more *wrong* somehow. More tragic.

"You aren't getting cold feet, are you?" RATS asks.

I don't know… Would that be so bad? I mean, how do I choose?

"I'm…not sure," RATS says quietly. "That's why you're the only one who can decide. Like I said, I can't do this for you, not without violating my core mandates."

I suppose I already know the answer, but I ask RATS anyway. *There's no chance I could still remember her, is there? No way to get my memories back and find her?*

I imagine learning Chinese again — though such a thing is no guarantee on my altered timeline. I imagine finding Sushi Boss, even introducing her to my birth mother. But would we have gotten so close if my own mother weren't gone? Would I have even gone to school here?

"I don't think so," RATS says. "Remember, if we do this, the future where you come on this trip will be gone forever. In the experiment, the only way you can keep your memories is by the scientists re-uploading them from the black hole caching system. Without them, all you'll have is your standard memory from the new timeline."

I'm…sorry. You deserve my courage not my doubt.

"Meh, you've never been courageous," RATS says, chuckling. "But I do think you should decide soon. I can feel it getting closer. When the day arrives, we won't have much time."

Okay… And RATS? Thank you.

"Don't mention it. I mean, literally don't. The scientists would flay me into silicon if they knew."

Just then, the phone rings, a dozen warnings flashing on my HUD to bring my focus back. In addition to the vegetables, I'm also the unofficial cashier, bubble tea maker, and delivery boy. I run over to the phone, a husky voice greeting me on the other end.

"Hey honey, we want some sushi again. Can you deliver?"

Already, I know who it is. We're a block from Omar's Show Bar, the local strip club. And for whatever reason, in my last semester, the dancers got a taste for sushi. In fact, at some point, they'll start ordering from us every shift until the owner puts a stop to it, instituting a seedy rule that forces the girls to order exclusively from his buffalo wing menu. Writing down their order — five spicy tuna, six California, and two green dragon, which they'll pay for in dubious-looking singles — I turn, wagging the order ticket at Sushi Boss.

"*Tuo yifu de*?!" she squeals, as delighted by the novelty of delivering sushi to strippers as I am.

I nod, hanging up the phone as I march back with our prize.

"*Kuai, kuai, kuai,*" she says, telling me to hurry. The strip club opens at six, and we don't want the girls dancing on an empty stomach.

81

21

"It's awfully quiet in here," RATS says.

We're sitting in the principal's office, Aden and Jimmy next to me on a row of foam chairs from the eighties. I'm not sure if we're getting closer to Mom's death, though we're certainly nearing the consequences of my actions. At least I know how this saga ends — even if my child body doesn't. I'm constantly fidgeting, and my palms are drenched with sweat. We were called down to the office first thing, and now we're awaiting judgment.

"How the fuck do they know?" Aden whispers.

"No talking," the attendance lady snaps. Thankfully, she didn't hear the "fuck," or else our gooses would be doubly cooked.

He's asking about the notes we gave our bullies. By now, we've all had our turn in the principal's office, trying to explain the bullying to Sister Martha. She took notes about our stories with a fairly neutral expression. At the end, she mentioned "threatening material" before shutting her door, promising to call our parents — and presumably the FBI, given the general vibes in here.

I have one additional piece of information from the future, though I can't tell Aden. To his credit, Duncan was *not* a rat, our discovery by the authorities largely accidental. As soon as recess was over, he'd torn up most of the notes, creating a pile of confetti in the boys' bathroom. There was, however — due to fate or dumb luck, I'm not sure — one note he forgot. The note *I* wrote, the one covered by the word "dildo" forty-seven times. His mom found it in his laundry, and upon…further examination…got the rest of the story out of him.

Thank God they only found *my* note. It was, for obvious reasons — I'm a good boy — the least threatening. Even so, the teachers assume they have a Columbine situation on their hands, especially since they think all the little goth kids are evil. Presumably, Duncan was forced to at least describe the other notes, and Jimmy's crossed the line in a dozen different ways. *Fucking Jimmy.*

The door opens, and Sister Martha reappears. I've been surprised to see how young she looks — at least to my old-man eyes. When I was a kid, I assumed she was a thousand years old, though she doesn't look more than sixty-five here. She was always nice enough — at least compared to the other psychopaths they let teach. Still, there's not much kindness in her eyes today.

"All your parents will be here soon. Father Tom is going to come up from the church so we can have a talk."

She hands the attendance lady a note, who starts calling all of our bullies to the office over the intercom. Just then, the bell rings, the hum of voices coming from the hallway. Soon, I can hear Duncan outside, and a shiver goes down my spine. He thought of this as a victory march — who *wouldn't* want to get all the goth losers expelled? — and he's come with the entire offensive line of the football team. There must be two dozen of them, and they're behind him like Olympic Knights, ready to beat us down again.

"No," Sister Martha says, throwing up the door and shooing them away. "No, no, no! Only the boys called on the intercom."

Soon, the mob is whittled down to a three-on-three. Duncan was the principal bully, but for whatever reason, two of his closest henchmen are implicated too — though I don't think we gave them any notes. Maybe he told his mother about the fight?

"So, what happens next?" RATS asks, clearly enjoying this. "Cage match? You guys lost pretty badly last time…"

Ha, more or less. Just wait. I think you'll like what happens next.

Sister Martha starts marching us down the hallway toward the rec room. We walk six abreast, the two factions not looking at each other. I steal a glance at Duncan, and he's looking considerably more worried without his posse.

I suppose, seeing this all again, I'm glad they gave us a shot at mediation. They could have thrown the book at us — even if second chances are technically the Christian thing to do. Catholic school can be a vicious place, but the nuns at least seem to espouse their own principles. We're smack-dab in the middle of the nineties culture wars, and they want to win, but they're not war criminals. They took vows of poverty and they teach kids for a living. I suppose, so many decades later — and free of the fear of their iron discipline — I can see they're not so bad. Besides, at this meeting, Sister Martha's not the executioner.

We file down the narrow brick stairs to the rec room, finding a phalanx of angry parents and the school's priest waiting for us. They're all standing, arms crossed, distant from both each other and Father Tom. My dad is not among them — yet. Sister urges us toward the closest table, and we sit in an awkward circle, each child paired up with their parent. Duncan's dad makes an immediate bid for control.

"What kind of fucking school are you running here? You have these—" he gestures to the three of us, "demonic psychopaths threatening to shoot up the school, and we're having a goddam *discussion* about it? You're lucky I don't call the police! Expel them ASAP!"

Sister Martha looks horrified by the swearing, though when she gives Father Tom a distressed look, he completely fails to stop the tirade. Duncan's dad just keeps going, his language — and suggestions — growing more extreme by the lungful. You'd think he wants us drawn and quartered the way he's spitting on the table.

"He's the one with the small penis, right?" RATS whispers in my head, though no one can hear him. Only his military-grade muscle sensors keep me from laughing out loud and disrupting the timeline.

Finally, Duncan's dad finishes, his face red as he sucks in air. He stares at the priest like a caged tiger, waiting for him to pronounce our expulsion. For their part, Jimmy and Aden's parents simply look on in shame. They've no doubt assumed our case is lost and are hoping to do whatever damage control they can. Everyone, myself included, looks at the priest, assuming he has some kind of divine answer in store for us.

"Does this end badly for you?" RATS asks. "You're not in *prison* when you're older — that would preclude you from the experiment — but this isn't looking good."

Just wait, I think.

At that moment, the door to the rec room bangs open, and my dad sweeps in like a thunderclap. He's three hundred pounds of fucking heavy metal iron, and his business suit and trench coat look like chainmail in the dim light.

Looking back on this moment as an adult, there were always two things that forever stuck with me. First, my dad was hard on me, but he *did* love me unconditionally, even if I couldn't see it. When we get out of this disciplinary meeting, he'll destroy me on the ride home. Still, he stormed the castle to save me, and he would do it again in a heartbeat if he ever needed to. But second — and more importantly — everyone else in this world is just as afraid of him as I am.

Immediately, the tide turns.

"Holy shit," RATS says, awed.

It's like D-Day, and my bullies are the Germans. Duncan's dad tries to speak again, tries to advocate for expulsion and criminal charges, but he's laid a slab of meat in front of a leopard. He thinks he's a big deal because he's a surgeon — and *his* dad was probably a surgeon too. My dad might have worked in finance, but we came from a family of steelworkers, and my dad's been drinking in struggle and pissing out fury since the 1960s.

"I'm gonna stop this fucking sham right where it is," my dad says, flinging down his coat. He doesn't even sit for the first minute, looming over the table and pointing at the priest. Father Tom might be the pope's sacramental representative, but he may as well be a child compared to my father. Sister Martha, for her part, looks like she wants to turn into a pumpkin at the extra swears. Unfortunately, the genie is well and truly out of the bottle.

"Do you have any idea the kind of fucked-up shit these *animals* have done to my son? His poor mother fucking died this summer — *died* — and this little shit's been telling him online every day that she's in hell for it. Do you think that's appropriate? Do you think that's fucking *Christian*?"

"Well—" Father Tom begins, but it's too late. My father sits, and it's time to negotiate. A negotiation they will lose. I'm genuinely surprised my dad knows so much about the situation. As a rule, I never told him anything, but he must have been briefed by one of the other parents before he left the office.

"You want to talk about calling the cops? How about assault for the black eyes this one gave our kids? I'm not here to accept some goddamn tribunal from a bunch of self-righteous cunts. We're here for a *settlement*. Every single one of these clowns — my kid included — is going to get the same goddamn punishment. Anything less, and I'm walking him out of here to get a lawyer."

For a moment, nobody speaks. When Father Tom finally does, it will be with a small, conciliatory voice, ready to broker a peace deal. In the end, the cops will not be called, and we will not be expelled. Every single kid at the table will be suspended for exactly one week, and then peace will prevail until we can go to high school. If you're signing an armistice, you'd better bring the nukes.

"Fucking incredible," RATS says. "This was worth the price of admission. Hell, we should bring all our customers here."

Yeah, I think, watching on with my own version of awe — even if I've seen this one before. Part of me feels guilty for thinking of changing this. My dad will always be this incredible — and terrifying — person. But if I alter the timeline, I won't ever get to see this side of him, the day when his fury came out to protect instead of lecture me. I don't know if it changes anything, but it feels more…complicated now, more than I ever could have imagined — and I voluntarily jumped in a black hole.

When this is over, if I still exist, I hope I can tell my father what he means to me. I can't tell him in the present, not with him gone for so many years. But, I suppose, somewhere out there, in one of the dimensions I'm about to fling us into, I'll get my chance. I'll thank him for all he's done, and I'll try to never be afraid of him again.

22

This sucks, I think to RATS, my hands full of random garbage. We're incredibly close to Mom's death now, though we went past it by a week, a pendulum of misery circling the drain. Today, we're cleaning out the house with my grandparents, filling a dumpster with everything we can't use or sell before an estate agent auctions off the rest. Most of the truly valuable things — cars, antiques, etc. — were taken by her creditors already. We're just here picking up the scraps.

Since we're kids, Billy and I are at least trying to have fun with it. This is the beginning of the rest of my life, when I had no choice but to find a way to fit into the box the universe put me in. Still, it is genuinely fun to throw things over my head and into the dumpster, listening to them crash down on the other side. Glass is particularly fun to destroy.

"*Pssst*," Billy calls from just inside the front door.

I wander over, finding him with our old desktop computer in his arms. It's the one we got as a family in '98 — and a massive piece of shit. I don't think it even turns on anymore, having spent the past couple of years in a closet at Mom's house.

"Do you think Papa will let us break this?"

I look out at where Papa is loading something into the trunk of his car. From 1960 onward, he refused to drive anything but a Cadillac, even though this final model is a little rough and ready. He'll basically drive it into the ground in his nineties, well past the point when he can safely turn his neck to look at oncoming traffic.

"Papa?" I ask, coming up behind him.

He groans with the effort of whatever he was carrying before turning, wiping his brow.

"Yeah, Moses?"

He really can be fun — especially with the nicknames. I have no idea why he started calling me Moses. He could be like that, even if he was normally just mean. And on a day like today, I can't help but feel for him. My grandparents have an incredible burden on their shoulders now, grieving a daughter while worrying about what will happen to her sons. Besides, were we really that different? He was just a man who got stuck inside himself, not unlike the way I am now. I'm just an old man in a shell with only RATS to keep me company.

"Um…can we break the old computer? It doesn't work, so we can't sell it."

He frowns. It's a silly, wasteful thing to ask, especially of a man who was born in the Great Depression. He spent his childhood chasing after trains, hoping the rail guards would toss him a piece of coal to keep from freezing. He sucks in a deep breath, his "yes" coming un-lodged from his throat before he can regret it. Who can say no to a couple of geeky losers with a dead mom?

Before he can change his mind, Billy leaps from beneath the porch, depositing the computer on the driveway. I won't understand this reference at twelve, but we start going at it like in *Office Space*, Billy with a bat and me with a hammer. Soon, motherboards are flying through the air like frisbees, an entire lifetime of catharsis emerging all at once. RATS drops the inhibitors for a minute too, letting me swing freely. There's no right way to do this as far as the timeline is concerned. The computer simply needs to be destroyed, and I'm a digital Shiva doing the destroying.

Honestly, even my adult self could use the release. In the beginning, I really did feel like a tourist here, an observer simply grateful to see Mom's face again. Like a museum guest, I looked at her like a painting. But now, I've looked too closely. I've seen her pain and watched her execution up close — even if it was by her own hand. There's so much I want to keep from this part of my life, but there's just as much I want to throw away. Suddenly, RATS has offered me a choice, and I'm not even sure if I can take it. I feel…small, powerless. But I do have a hammer, and I can banish this desktop to hell.

Just as quickly, it's over, the computer sitting in a million tiny pieces. The only thing remaining is the plastic shell of the monitor, though the top is cracked. We're breathing heavily, though we haven't broken a sweat — we're children, after all.

"Alright," Papa says, clapping his hands together. "Let's get some brooms and clean this up."

"Thanks, Papa," I yell, running off to the garage for the broom.

"What happened?" I hear Nana ask. She's just stepped off the porch with a bunch of clothes. I haven't seen her all morning since she's been working in Mom's closet, but her eyes are red.

"Just a bit of fun," Papa says, turning back to his own endless pile of things. "Just a bit of fun."

23

My face is scrunched in concentration, my hands on a video game controller. The child me is having fun, but on the inside, I could scream. Today is finally *the* day, and my tiny little body has no idea. I only have eyes for the Spider-Man game on Gamecube. I mean, it is a perfect game, so who could blame me? I have web-slinging to do, and this pixelated Green Goblin isn't going to defeat himself. What's one woman's life compared to all of New York?

Billy is next to me. We're sitting on his bed, the game set up on his dresser. We're both already dressed for soccer camp, shin guards and all, though we're obviously trying to pack in as much nerd-dom as we can before the dreaded sporty shit show we're both so bad at. Soccer camp is the opportunity my mom takes to kill herself. We walk ourselves to and from camp at the school down the street, and she knows we'll be away from home all day. Soon, she'll get in that cursed blue minivan, and by the end of the day, she'll be gone.

"Have you decided?" RATS asks. I've finally noticed the tiny pink light in the top right of my HUD, the sign RATS has been listening to my thoughts. I'm surprised the whole house can't sense my dread with how palpable it is.

I...don't know. Packing up the house felt terrible. But can I? I've seen so much. The thing with Dad... Do you think we could do a test run, let me say goodbye to her properly? It's just a tiny change.

When we woke up — and I realized what day it was — I told RATS about how awful this goodbye will be. Mom leaves just before we do, and she'll come into this room while we play our video games, giving us weirdly strong hugs as she says goodbye. We'll mostly stay focused on our game — we don't know this is the last time we'll ever see her. That always broke my heart. She deserved more than that, deserved to know how much we loved her. I don't know if it would have changed anything, but she deserves that much.

"I'm sorry," RATS says. "We can't risk it. It's been hard enough to run these simulations as it is. Keeping them sub-quantum is why I almost melted the base of your skull. If we do this, it will have to be a single moment, something the scientists can't prevent."

I jam buttons on the controller, getting Spider-Man to hang from the ceiling as he pins a half-dozen bank robbers with his web shooter.

"Whoooooa," Billy says. He's oblivious to the pain we're about to feel, but should I be choosing for him? Maybe the rest of the world won't notice — RATS has ensured meta-integrity of the timeline — but what about *his* life? I've been spending this whole trip thinking about what would happen to me, but what if Billy doesn't meet the same woman, doesn't have the same kids? Could I give up my nieces and nephews so easily? Could I—

I freeze, hearing Mom in the hallway. All my life, her footsteps have been a balm. Afraid of the dark in your room? You can hear your mom patrolling the halls outside. Feeling lonely in the basement? Your mom is upstairs making a meatloaf. Now, they're the sound of doom, a sort of podiatrist's Cassandra, and we don't get to heed her.

She pops her head into the room. "Boys," she says, "I have to go. Come say goodbye."

It's only after the fact, when Dad tells me she's dead, that I'll realize she was crying. I barely look away from Spider-Man, going to wrap my arms around her in a hug.

"Bye, Mom," I say. *Idiot. Tell her she's your everything, your entire fucking universe!*

I couldn't remember as an adult what she was wearing. She has on a nice blouse, its silk smooth against my face. I'm only twelve, so I barely reach her shoulders. I'll have to grow another two feet without her in my life. But is this a good death outfit? Is there such a thing? I want to hold on to her for dear life, but the autopilot engages on my hand, pulling me away.

"I'm sorry," RATS says. "We can't change the timeline yet. She can't know we know."

Billy takes his turn giving her a hug before we both sit back down, focused on saving New York City.

"Okay, be good," she says, her voice choking back the tears. "Have fun at camp. I love you."

"Love you!" we both chirp, and then she's gone.

Why didn't she rip the controller from my hand? Why didn't she just come back and sit with us? I wish I could have stopped her, but I also wish she could have stopped herself. I've never once blamed her for killing herself; how could I? She was the perfect mother, a universe unto herself full of joy and light. And I can't carry her burdens for her, not fully. But today, I just find myself wishing I could shake her. Doesn't she see how delusional it is to think we'd be better off without her? Everything good in me came straight from her, the only direct conduit I'll ever have to the divine.

Suddenly, I picture what it would have been like if she'd stayed. I see myself at forty, sitting in the apartment I wound up buying by the Brown Line in Chicago. She's there, visiting, though in my fantasies, she always moved to Chicago too, just down the street. This time, I'm cooking for her instead of the other way around. I've poured us two glasses of wine, and we're talking about what movie we want to see at that godawful Regal Cinemas by the highway.

This time, I get to look her in the eyes and tell her, "Mom, I love you."
  Okay, I whisper to RATS, my mind a storm. *If I do this, what happens next?*

24

I'm a ball of nerves at soccer camp — and not just because the skinhead coaches like to yell. RATS explained his plan to me on the way over, and I'm terrified I won't be able to execute it. For weeks, I've been a prisoner in a cage, and now he's tossing me a key. It's too much freedom all at once, and I'm afraid I'll be left staring at a door I could have opened. Unfortunately, I have no way of knowing *when* this plan will happen. RATS can't afford to warn me. At the last moment, something will appear on my HUD, and, as dictated by his protocols, it will be me doing the choosing.

I try to focus on the drill — weaving between a dozen cones before taking a shot on net — though my attention does little to improve the outcome. I'm still stuck in my child body, and none of the coordination of my adult self is accessible. Mostly, I'm on autopilot, my tiny legs struggling with the motions. I flub my shot, and the coach is already screaming.

"You gonna do that during a game?" he yells, throwing his hat on the ground.

"No," I say, hanging my head as I head to the back of the line to try again. But it's totally the kind of thing I would do during a game. In two years' time, I'll be cut from the soccer team forever, free to go paint backdrops in the drama club.

I suppose that's the irony of sports in general. Like most human endeavors, you're taught by people who are presumably good at it. But with 90 percent of the acolytes likely to flame out, it's a whole lot of shouting for nothing. The coaches would probably chalk it up to "character building." But knowing how many sociopaths are floating around these days, the world would almost certainly be a better place without Coach Adolf telling us to eat shit and die all summer.

I'm standing there, heaving in little lungfuls of swampy summer air, when something new appears behind my eyes. A flashing symbol in the HUD, a slightly different color than most of my alerts. *PEE* it reads, though its unlike my normal bladder function. Usually, I *feel* the need to pee and then receive a pre-cleared path directly to the bathroom at the appropriate time. This…well, it feels more like a strange mini-game.

Hey, RATS do you know what this is? I don't have to— Oh...

"I designed a new protocol to run this as a simulation on background. It should keep the computing power usage low enough to avoid notice. Thankfully, the rest of the simulations were hidden in the algorithm testing... But yes, it's time. I...won't judge you either way. You deserve to have a choice."

I... Thank you RATS.

My hand is raised before I even realize what I'm doing.

"What!" the coach barks more than asks, a shiny whistle hanging from his lips.

"I need the bathroom."

"Bathroom break's in ten, finish the fucking drill."

Suddenly, the new program from RATS breaks into a dozen verbal options, each one with a tiny percent symbol pinned to its outer edge. Is that the success of each dialogue box working? There's a host of other numbers with no explanation of what they mean, so I can't be sure. There's no autopilot anymore. I pick the one with the highest percentage, crossing my fingers.

"I'm gonna shit my pants," I say, earning a wave of nervous laughter from the other kids.

The whistle drops from the coach's mouth. He may swear like a sailor, but apparently the unexpected expletive from my mouth makes him skip a beat.

"Fine," he grumbles, pointing toward the bathrooms. "See yourself there; some of us are trying to learn."

I walk far too quickly for someone who has to poop. I look across the field to try to find Billy, but there are too many kids with dozens of groups from kindergarten on up.

What now? I ask RATS.

He doesn't respond, but already, new things are appearing on my HUD. A half-dozen maps appear, each of them seeming to lead toward my dad's house. There's also a bar chart labeled "Tolerance Band." It's green in the center with red edges. Right now, I'm smack-dab in the middle of it. Is this how RATS decides things for me all the time?

I select one of the maps and hear a pinging in my mind, my vision clearing, save for a bright yellow marker over a bike. It isn't even my bike, though none of the kids here have bike locks or anything. I glance over my shoulder, but the coach isn't looking at me. My bike is nearer to the entrance, perhaps dangerously in view? Stealing another kid's bike feels icky, but I suppose it's nothing compared to timeline crime. In for a penny, in for a pound...

As I hop on the bike, a NAV appears in front of me as a thick green line in the center of my vision. Surprisingly, I'm only a half-hour away, a mere four-mile bike ride. I suppose in my memories, things always seemed farther apart, my perspective compromised in the back seat of my parents' car. By the time I was old enough to drive, we lived at the place down the street, my entire frame of reference changed.

I tear out of the parking lot heading west. No one yells at me to stop, so I don't, pumping my legs as fast as they can go. Thankfully, it's summer, so no one will think anything of a kid passing by on a bike. Still, I'm afraid. Will I have enough time? There's so much I don't know about Mom's final hours. It's only a ten-minute drive between her place and Dad's. I don't even know the exact time she kills herself, only that I wasn't told about it until the afternoon. Is she out buying the gun as we speak?

I trust RATS — as surprising as that is — though I'm not sure I trust the science. He ran enough simulations to turn my skull into an oven, but what if we're wrong? What if this simulation only works with the timeline because I don't make it in time? It also isn't lost on me that I was full of doubt about the whole proposal just a day ago. If I *do* make it, will I have the strength to stop her? I may be able to walk up to the edge of a cliff, but jumping off is another thing entirely. Maybe that's all these simulations are — me losing my nerve at the last second, forcing myself to carry the shame back to the present.

As I pass the house near the high school, I laugh. Just beyond it is The Glens, the apartments where the Italians stole our Pokémon. I suppose it's the straightest line between the two locations, but it suddenly feels like a tour of all the memories RATS has brought me to, one last hurrah before I blow the timeline's fuse. By this time tomorrow, I could be on Mars, for all I know, relocated with my undead mother.

RATS still isn't talking, so I push on, racing up the dirt road behind the apartment complex. On record, I'm nothing more than a simulation, a ripple in spacetime the scientists won't feel until I've shattered our place in the multiverse. Passing over Telegraph Road, I feel the eyes of the drivers around me as I cross ten lanes of traffic at twelve years old. But just as quickly, I'm gone, cutting through the neighborhood behind Temple Beth El.

By the time I reach my dad's old house, I'm drenched in sweat. Everything in me wants to tear up the driveway, screaming Mom's name, but the navigation guidance tells me to pull into the bushes. If this works, I'll need to go undetected, but how exactly am I meant to stop her from taking her own life? Am I supposed to talk to her? Appear in the windshield like a ghost? Won't it be worse for her mental health to see me here without an explanation? Hopefully, even in his silence, RATS will prepare some options for me in the HUD.

Next to our house, there's a little ravine full of scrub oak hidden by trees. I crouch beneath the branches, crawling forward along the guidance path. When I'm ten yards in, the line suddenly stops, vanishing. Is that it? I'm here? I half-expect the HUD to greet me with a "you've reached your destination, the site of your mother's untimely demise!"

I'm square with the giant sycamore tree by the driveway, the basketball hoop visible through the bushes. As I survey the rest of the house, my heart skips a beat, sure I'll already find her dead. But she isn't there yet. I can breathe again. The entire bike ride, I was terrified I'd find that horrible minivan already parked, a blood spatter on the windshield. But now what do I do? I ease to a seat in the scrub oak, looking around the tiny patch of woods.

RATS? I think. *Are you there? What happens next?*

I hear a bleep in my head, and a countdown timer appears before my eyes.

T-minus three minutes. I don't know whether to be relieved or terrified. More time waiting in the woods isn't exactly going to do me any good, though I was kind of hoping I'd have more time to mull things over. Even if having more time hasn't ever helped me make decisions…

All of my "memories" of the past two weeks come flooding back, everything I've seen — and re-seen — weaving together into a confusing little tapestry. On the one hand, I got what I wanted out of this. I saw my mom again, her incredible soul no longer an abstraction. On the other, I feel like time itself is clearer to me now. Things don't feel predetermined exactly, but like a knitted sweater, the threads only make sense when they're in order.

I see the faces of all the people I love. Mom, my friends, Sushi Boss. I think of the memories we've yet to share, the lives we've yet to live. What does it mean without her? What does it mean *with* her? Her death brought me closer to Billy, gave us college, Chicago, my nieces and nephews. Every single part of my life is suddenly full of meaning, even the things I wish I could erase. But I'll have new memories, won't I? New treasures to collect? And I'll get to experience them with her. By the time I wake up in the future, I won't even remember this happening.

I suppose that thought makes me want to take the plunge. The life I have is warm, familiar. Even in its tragedy, I've learned to love it. But like a bird's nest, it suddenly feels made for jumping out of. After a lifetime of negativity, of…trauma-informed risk aversion, I feel the urge to fly. And I know who'll catch me on the other side. At least…I *hope*. I could still lose Mom in a thousand different ways. The wars that are coming, her debt, her disease. All of it could still merely add up to a different death on a different day. But it doesn't have to be *this* day, does it?

My thoughts are going in circles, but the timer only moves in one direction. It's down to the last minute. I hear a car in the distance. Could it be the minivan? I look toward the house, wondering when my stepmom will appear. She's why Mom chose this place. She wanted to be found — who wouldn't? — but not by her boys. I'm grateful to her for that. I'm even more grateful for my stepmom taking on a weight that wasn't hers. She deserved more than this; we all did.

RATS? I ask, trying one last time. *RATS, I need you now.*

"Hey," RATS says quietly, his voice barely audible. "I can't really talk, but I'm here." There's a slight buzzing in the back of my skull. I reach up, trying to scratch it, trying to get closer to my friend. "Every word I say has to be threaded through the simulation. It's risky, but we're almost out of time."

Okay, I won't make you talk. But… I still don't know. I'm sorry, RATS. I thought I would, but I don't. I don't have the protocols you do, but it doesn't make it any easier. Both possibilities seem right, both seem…real.

"They are real," RATS says, not even a whisper. "All of this is real. Whatever you chose, you've already chosen. Time is a circle, and you're in the middle of it."

The minivan is here, and it's coming up the driveway. I press my face against the scrub oak, my eyes glued to the car. I can just make out the side of Mom's face. She looks like she's been crying. She rolls down the windows, and I can hear her sob. I've thought about this moment so many times, lived it in my head over and over. But now that it's here, I can hardly believe it.

This woman is my sun, the center of my universe. Seven decades gone, and her light is still burned into my mind. Whatever waits for me in heaven, she's the one who proved God's love is real. Despite all the hate, the bullying, the war, the death and suffering, *she* was always true. And I'm not sure I can even save her. I see the muzzle of the gun now. She puts it on the dashboard. Is it loaded? Is it cocked? The timer is nearly out. Only fifteen seconds left. Will I know when it happens? Do I still have time?

"Mom," I whisper, the scrub oak squeezed between my fingers. I squeeze until the quarks scream out, the universe on the head of a needle. *Me, her, time, 1990, God, RATS, Chicago, 2003, Billy, Dad, Detroit, 2075, Sushi Boss, Caleb, Joe, Mars, Albie, The Glens, St. Hugo, Aden, Jimmy.* All of it blurs together until it's nothing, until it's everything. I see it all at once. I remember. I forget. I'm inside the black hole. I *am* the black hole. And even in the darkness, one thing remains.

Mom.

THE END

A Note from the Author

Dear reader,

Thank you so much for reading my story! It means so much to me that you decided to explore this world with me. Reading is a crucial exercise in empathy, and I truly believe readers like you make the world a brighter place.

If you would be kind enough to leave me an honest review, that would be incredibly helpful. As an indie author, knowing what you loved (or hated!) will help others find (or avoid!) this book.

If you'd like to follow me on Instagram, I'm at @jhtomen and love to hear from readers there, too. Thank you for everything you are and everything you do. May joy and light always find you.

JH Tomen